A Farebrother

The Sedgeborough World

A novel. Vol. 1

A Farebrother

The Sedgeborough World
A novel. Vol. 1

ISBN/EAN: 9783337213558

Printed in Europe, USA, Canada, Australia, Japan

Cover: Foto ©Andreas Hilbeck / pixelio.de

More available books at **www.hansebooks.com**

THE
SEDGEBOROUGH WORLD.

A Novel.

By A. FAREBROTHER.

IN TWO VOLUMES.—VOL. I.

There's a divinity that shapes our ends,
Rough hew them how we will.

LONDON:
SAMUEL TINSLEY, 34, SOUTHAMPTON ST., STRAND.
1872.

I Dedicate

THIS AND WHATEVER WORK I MAY DO IN THE FUTURE

To Her

WHO, THOUGH NOW REMOVED FROM THIS WORLD OF SORROW,

STILL IS, AS SHE EVER HAS BEEN, THE MOTIVE POWER

OF ALL MY WORK;

AND WITH HER NAME I JOIN THAT

Of One

WHO HAS SHARED ALL MY LESSONS AND EXPERIENCES.

CHAPTER I.

" The curtains see
Dividing. She is there."

IT was said by every one in Sedgeborough
that Florence Aylmer was appallingly intellectual. This was thought most amusing by
her own family, and no one supposed that as
she laughed at it herself she was in the least
pained. But what we possess we either
overrate or undervalue; and while ordinary
girls heard of her with envy, Florence would
have given much to have been considered an
ordinary girl, and to have escaped the
charge of being intellectual.

B

It was a source of never-failing wonder to
her how it came about that the charge was
made. She listened with amazement to the
witticisms, lively talk, and delicately-worded
sarcasms which fell naturally from the lips of
other women, and felt their authors inspired
her with a certain dread. Yet she saw these
sought after and courted on all sides, while
she, who was never sarcastic or severe, was
avoided by most men and women of her own
age. The only solution of the problem at
which she could arrive was, that she could
never speak without seriously meaning what
she said, and involuntarily led conversation
to literary subjects. She envied the talent
which enabled others to talk for hours in
lively and amusing strains, and all about
nothing. For her own part, she found after
a conversation with any one, she had always
given and drawn forth thought; while her
mother, and her sister Lois, a girl still in

the school-room, would not in the same time have penetrated beneath the surface, and would have been pleasant and amusing without having said anything which could be remembered afterwards.

Florence was painfully aware that it is a great mistake to treat of a serious subject in general conversation, and yet time after time she fell into the mistake, and constantly exposed the woeful ignorance of her interlocutor, much to their mutual confusion.

Thus it was she gained the reputation of being appallingly intellectual.

She was not accomplished, like other girls who were yet called commonplace, and of whom no one was afraid. She could neither play nor sing a note—music, indeed, was often a positive pain to her. She had learnt to draw to please her father, who wished her to do something like other women; but then not even the most partial critic could call her drawings more than tolerable.

She declared that some day she would fall from her pinnacle, and be found out to be a pitiful pretender, and then she would be treated with ignominy, " which will be very hard, as I am sure it is no pleasure to me to be placed up here," she said woefully.

Her elder sister, Lizzie, laughed when she heard this; for she was perfectly satisfied in her own mind that Florence would never be proved to be a "pitiful pretender," and believed even more implicitly than others in her sister's intellectual powers.

From her face alone Florence would have gained the character of being intellectual.

It was a beautiful face. When seen in repose you thought you would wish her never to move; but when she smiled you wished the smile would always remain. The smile, however, was fleeting as it was sweet. It came apparently to provoke a desire to see it again. Her face was oval, while the dark blue eyes were full of thought and depth; and if you have seen Guido's Magdalene, you know the colour and the beauty of the hair, which was allowed to fall low over the broad forehead. She was about five feet nine inches in height, and moved with a serene grace and dignity, of which she was all un-conscious. The white, well-shaped, rather large hands, were indicative of a character somewhat devoid of practical activity or mechanical power.

When Florence was twelve, Mrs. Aylmer engaged a lady as governess to her children, whose sole delight was in scientific and philo-sophical studies. She had been attracted by Florence at once, and had devoted herself to the cultivation of an intellect which would, she believed, repay her by sympathy and comprehension. Up to this time Florence

had not been strong, and was much confined
to the house; and when the general work of
lessons was over, Miss Frost would proceed
to effect the proposed cultivation by reading
with her on subjects of which the generality
of women are almost ignorant. The strain
put on her mind during the day would often
leave Florence exhausted and worn out in
the evening, when, nevertheless, she had to
appear in the drawing-room and take the
part of a woman in conversation. Mrs.
Aylmer had doubted the advisability of this
method of education, but had hesitated so
long before taking steps to put an end to it,
that finally these steps were never taken.
But as Florence's mind was strong and
healthy, this over-exertion did not leave the
evil effects that might have been anticipated,
and now, at the age of eighteen, she was quite
capable of being a companion to Miss Frost,
who still remained as governess to Lois.

Florence's claims to being considered intellectual were, therefore, these:—She could
read and speak German and French fluently,
and was well read in the classical and modern
literature of both countries, as well as in that
of her own; for Mrs. Aylmer had herself
directed her daughter's English studies, which
no one was better qualified than she to
do. Florence moreover could have passed a
fair examination in Greek and Latin.

Her historical studies had left her mind
a blank as to dates; but the social and
political conditions of the different nations
were familiar to her; and I would beg of
you only to think how pleasant it would
be if we could only say the same.

She was well versed in the theories main-
tained by the different philosophical teachers
of ancient and modern times, from Thales
to Comte; and, above all, she could have
enlightened you as to the undulatory theory

of light, radiation, the colour and structure
of the sky, and the polarization of its light,
—and would have found pleasure in so doing.
I fear had her godfathers and godmothers
inquired into her religious doctrines, they
would hardly have been satisfied. She could
not say more of the Apostles' Creed than the
first clause; but she did say that clearly,
firmly, and truthfully,—so truthfully, indeed,
that any weakening of her faith would have
darkened the world to her. In her mind,
moreover, might have been found the ele-
mental constituents of all true religion—-
reverence, awe, truth, and love.

There were some people, who were nearly
enough related to have a right to be dis-
agreeable, who told Mrs. Aylmer that she had
brought up her family badly, and that,
having sown the wind, she must expect to
reap the whirlwind. Mrs. Aylmer had borne
all such prophecies with wonderful equani-

mity, being secretly well satisfied with her
own progeny.

Her eldest son, Sydney, had done well at
school, and had now gained golden opinions
at Oxford, where he had just taken a good
fellowship. Mr. Aylmer, who had always
declared that Sydney was too fond of re-
finements and subtleties ever to do much,
was obliged to admit that he had every
cause for satisfaction. Sydney had wished
to study medicine, but his father, who
seldom interfered with the tastes and
wishes of his children, put a direct veto
on this.

"He would not have any son of his a
dirty drug-maker."

"The noblest profession there is," murmured Sydney; but he was young then,
and submitted, which he would not have
done had he been called on to decide the
question now that he was two-and-twenty

years of age. He was of a naturally independent disposition, and none of his people
knew much of his plans, occupations, or
thoughts. He wrote to his mother when he
had anything of importance to say, and
prided himself on these short notes being
direct and to the point. He was not intimate with any of his sisters, as he looked
upon women as curious and unsatisfactory
phenomena. But since they were evils
necessary to the conditions of life, he would
have inculcated on them the old nursery
rhyme—

> Speak when you are spoken to,
> Do as you are bid ;
> Shut the door after you,
> And you'll never be chid.

The women-kind, therefore, belonging to
him did not at all conform to his ideas of
what was suitable; and having found it
vanity and vexation of spirit to endeavour
to teach them their true position in the

scheme of creation, he avoided them generally when at home. For Lizzie, indeed, he had some regard, "for she had pretensions to good sense, and an idea, though indistinct, of the fitness of things," and he would condescend to notice her occasionally, as a sign of his approval. He thought Florence a monstrosity; and as for Lois, she should be kept in the nursery, and be put on a course of bread and water till the sharp edge was taken off her tongue. At all this his mother smiled, and thought he "was young enough yet, poor boy; but he would be bitten more severely than others when his time came." For Mrs. Aylmer looked on falling in love as a disease which all men must have sooner or later, as their dogs have distemper.

Her daughter Lizzie Mrs. Aylmer also felt to be very satisfactory. She was not clever, it is true, "but then, poor thing, she is so sensible." Mrs. Aylmer could rely on her to be always ready at the right moment, and always to say the right thing. She could entertain all the dull and commonplace people, such as heavy young men, from whom Mrs. Aylmer's brightest sallies could not draw forth a spark, and who, when turned over to Lizzie, were metamorphosed into very pleasant, agreeable companions. Moreover, though Lizzie's features were by no means classical or delicately chiselled, her rich brown hair, fair face, and bright cheeks, made her look quite pretty. She had a sweet voice also, and had learnt enough music to be able to play simple accompaniments to her singing on the piano.

Lois was most like her mother of any of her children in face and character, although her mental capabilities would never equal those of Mrs. Aylmer. Lois was thirteen years of age, was dark-haired, dark-eyed,

and vivacious, to whom Miss Frost found it a
vain attempt to endeavour to teach what she
had taught Florence. She declared that
Hegel's theories were "lunatic," that she
could have invented better herself; and as for
the Institutes of Metaphysics, they were all
full of egoism, and she had enough of that
without it being brought into her lessons.
On the other hand, Huxley and Spencer
might be very well-meaning and very interesting for those who understood their
writings—she could not, that was all; and as
for Newton's apple, she believed it would
have fallen to the ground without any law of
gravitation, " for you see it grew ripe, and
then—why it fell, of course." She liked
reading " in moderation, you know," as long
as she read about things of which she could
afterwards talk with effect; for she could
not bear to be ignorant on any subject
which was talked of in her presence, and

had always something to say—whether that something was sensible or not, might be a question. Notwithstanding her contempt for Hegel, she was unwittingly a disciple of his, in so far that she believed that whatever she thought must be true. She would, for instance, give forth opinions on subjects of which she had never heard before, with an "it stands to reason, you know,"—which generally proved to be very convincing to the uninitiated.

The other remaining child, Charles, a boy of eight, had as yet shown no particular talent, except one for dirtying himself and his clothes on every occasion. It is true he had hinted with mysterious gravity, that probably when he grew to be a man he might become a butler where two footmen were kept, and was exceedingly hurt when this confidence was not treated with the consideration it deserved.

It was Mrs. Hamilton, the wife of her eldest brother, who had told Mrs. Aylmer most clearly, that she thought she was bringing up her family ill.

"No child of mine should speak until it is spoken to, before coming to years of discretion; nor should she mix freely in society, as yours do, Evelyn," she had said.

"But then, you see," replied Mrs. Aylmer with spirit, "my girls are not to be introduced into London society and make great marriages."

"I really think you should take them to London."

"Nonsense, Cornelia, you know as well as I that we could not afford it, and would not care about it if we could."

"I suppose you could not; but it is a pity."

"I don't see that. My girls will have very pleasant society in Sedgeborough, and

as much of it as will be good for them. I
am afraid when you have succeeded in getting
into London society, you will be hardly
repaid for your pains. At least, all the
Londoners that I have seen—and, thank
heaven, they have been few!—have either
been most ordinary people, or so heartily
tired of themselves and everybody else, 'that
I could have jumped like a school-girl when
I got away from them."

"Well, my dear Evelyn, as you say, you
have met few of them. But it is the way
you let your girls speak to you that I think
is not wise. Perhaps it is the fashion among
you Sedgeborough folks."

"As my girls are rational, I treat them
like rational beings; of course all girls could
not be treated in the same way," she said,
with meaning.

"Lois is becoming a regular little vixen,"
—and Mrs. Hamilton laughed. She and Mrs.

Aylmer never hesitated to use to each other any words that might occur to them; and when it suited her humour, no woman could speak with such unblushing insolence as Mrs. Hamilton. She would, however, have found many people to agree with her as to the way Mrs. Aylmer allowed her daughters to speak to her. She was much more like their sister, and when she spoke sharply to them, thought nothing of receiving a sharp reply. She did not deny that they had all quick and excitable tempers; but then it was her theory that a storm of thunder and lightning clears the air, and to be "liable to it" occasionally was, to her mind, infinitely preferable to living with a smouldering volcano. "Poor Dick," she said, thinking of her brother, "I would not be in his place for worlds."

Mr. Aylmer was a lawyer by profession, and was considered a most able man. He was very silent when at home, and though fond of his children, and proud of them, he left their management entirely to his wife. Therefore, the whole responsibility of their education fell upon her. "And I am sure I have a handful with you all," she said.

"Only mamma, dear," said Lois, "like a wise woman, you don't attempt to keep us in hand."

CHAPTER II.

"Their tongue is a sharp sword."

"Thought is the soul of act * * *
* * * * and incorporeally affects
The world producing deeds, but not by deeds."

"How provoking! Here is a letter from your Aunt Cornelia, saying she is coming to town this afternoon, will call here, and hopes to find some of us at home," said Mrs. Aylmer, impatiently, one afternoon on which she and her two eldest daughters were engaged to go to her mother-in-law's.

"Oh! mamma, take Lois with you, if Miss Frost will spare her, and let me stay at home," cried Florence; "we have been living in such a whirl of gaiety lately, I shall be quite glad of the holiday. I don't think Aunt Cornelia will stay long."

" It is very provoking. Cornelia's visits are like angels' only so far as they are few and far between; she always manages to time them badly. There are to be some very pleasant people at the old lady's."

" I assure you, mamma, I shall feel quite grateful to Aunt Cornelia, if she will only not stay long. I don't think, after all, that more than an hour's talk will be endurable about Mr. So-and-So, who is so charming, and is second son of a second son of a noble lord, or perhaps only of some honourable baronet."

" You are becoming quite sarcastic, Florence," laughed Lizzie. " If you go on·this way, you will soon show some of that appalling intellect about which we have all heard."

" Shall I go, then, mother," said Florence, rising, " and ask Miss Frost to spare Lois to go with you ?"

"Yes; and remember you must ask your aunt to stay. Say how much pleasure it would give me to see her, as I am sure I never could be so unblushing as to say it myself."

"And so you ask me to be unblushing for you? No, I thank you," answered Florence, smiling, as she left the room.

The school-room was up stairs, and when Florence came in, Lois was being examined in the history of Bysantium. Miss Frost granted leave for her to go with her mother, at which she collected her books gleefully, declaring that she was convinced "good, kind Miss Frost would not regret this, for she, Lois, was sure it would be much better for her to listen to her grandmother's experiences and wisdom, than to learn about 'dreadful, shocking women like the Empress Irene.'" This outburst did not draw a smile from the governess's face, and Florence laughingly bade her sister be gone, and be silent, and drawing a low chair to the fire, said, "I intend to enjoy the luxury of an idle aftenoon."

"Luxury?" questioned Miss Frost. "I hoped you might intend to read with me." Miss Frost spoke in low tones, but her voice was hard and grating. She was a woman whose appearance was called, even by her best friends, "unfortunate." Her complexion was swarthy, pallid, and unhealthy, while the shape of her face was square, from the square broad forehead to the square broad chin. Nature, moreover, seemed to have forgotten to give her a nose, until she had only sufficient material left to form an excuse for one, which hardly rose above the surface. Her teeth were large and prominent, being placed in her gums at long irregular intervals, so that when her lips were closed her mouth was distorted. Her hair was black and cut short, giving no relief to the short-

comings of her face, while her thick eyebrows ran across in straight lines. But it
was her eyes which beggared description.
They were large in size, and, if they had
any pretensions to colour, it was to a faint
green, much of the white being shown beneath and at each side of the pupil. It
always seemed as though she were looking
at you through a mist of thought, and from
a world far removed from yours. It must
be admitted that her face was as intellectual
and striking as it was unprepossessing.

Mr. Aylmer's daily prayer was, that Lois
might be emancipated from the school-room,
and Miss Frost dismissed. It was enough to
make a man cut his throat, he said, to be
forced to live with such an appearance,—her
eyes and teeth haunted him : he saw them
in his business-room, and he saw them in the
dark watches of the night.

"Good heavens!" he once exclaimed to

his wife; " what have I done to deserve such a fate?"

" As what?" she inquired, in surprise.

"As to be forced to live in the house with such an object."

Miss Frost's manners were cold, almost repellent; and people said of her, " She is an embodied Intellect, not a woman." But Florence could have told a different tale. She knew that Miss Frost's love was difficult to win; but, when once won, that no trials, however severe, would weaken its intensity. She had no affections which could be rightly or easily given away to all comers, for she knew too well that strangers were repelled by her for them to be anything but repellent to her. But for the one or two whom she did love, it would be no extravagance to say that she would go through fire and water for them.

Florence rose from her seat. " What a

reproof," she said. "I know though how I shall get into favour again;" and going to the bookcase, she brought out a new work by Helmholtz. "I shall read this to you," she continued.

She had not, however, been allowed to read much before a servant came to tell her that Mrs. Hamilton was in the drawing-room.

Helmholtz was put away hastily, for Florence knew that her aunt was a terrible person for any one lower than a countess to keep waiting.

"My dear Florence, how well you look!" was the greeting she received; "it was really good of Evelyn to leave me the flower of her flock. What! not forgotten to blush yet, though you have come out? Well, have the good folks of Sedgeborough been gay? Come, and tell me all about it."

Mrs. Hamilton was a tall, handsome

woman, who appeared hardly more than
thirty years of age. She was usually much
admired, but her features were hard, and
seemed as though they had been cut out of
wood. She was a woman who had never
known what it was to blush, and who allowed
the principles of truth to be no inconvenience
to her. She would have quite despised herself, had she allowed herself to be restrained
by anything so petty.

" How do you like being a come-out young
lady?" she continued, sitting beside Florence,
and surveying her in a cool, leisurely way,
as from an eminence.

" How did Agatha enjoy her season last
year?" asked Florence.

" Oh! immensely. Do you mean to say
we have not met since we went to London
last year? How strange!"

" Not very strange, I think. We were
abroad all last summer, and you seldom come

here. By the bye, mamma was obliged to go out; but she told me to tell you she hoped you would stay."

"Quite impossible! I have only come for a little indispensable shopping. I must be home this evening by seven o'clock, in time to dress for dinner. What do you say to coming out now, and giving me the help of your taste in my purchases?"

Florence rose with alacrity. She believed it would be infinitely preferable to go out shopping than to be shut up in the house with her Aunt Cornelia for a long tête-à-tête.

"You have not told me how you liked your balls," went on Mrs. Hamilton, as soon as they were out.

"I never dance; so I don't go to balls."

"Not dance? What's that for? Religious notions?"

"I do not like it."

"Perhaps you did not find the partners Sedgeborough could afford all that could be wished?"

"I have never been to a ball; but I should think men danced as well in Sedgeborough as anywhere else."

"Should you? You have had so much experience, you know."

"Well, I have not noticed any deformity about them, which would prevent their dancing well; but perhaps that may be from my Sedgeborough eyes." And Florence hated herself for having answered her aunt pettishly.

"It is a pity you could not go to London. Now you must tell me what milliners' shops you patronize, and what sort of wares they keep. Are they any way tolerable?"

Florence thought her mother would have said, "Oh, well enough for us good folks of Sedgeborough. I wonder you did not telegraph to London or Paris for what you wanted." She contented herself, however, with replying that she would take her aunt to the best shops, such as they were.

It was late before Mrs. Hamilton was satisfied with the goods shown her, and when Florence left her at the station, she was heartily and thoroughly tired of what she had hoped would prove a holiday. She had just time to prepare for dinner at seven. As they waited in the drawing-room for the guests to arrive, Mrs. Aylmer questioned Florence as to how she had enjoyed herself.

" Oh! mamma, she says I am the flower of your flock, and am to pay her a long visit soon," said Florence, and her face was very woeful.

" Well, you shall have Ernest Stuart to take you to dinner," laughed her mother. " His sister's brother must be clever, so I hope you may be rewarded by a pleasant evening."

"I don't think even being his sister's brother could redeem a curate from uninterestingness," said Lizzie.

The arrival of their friends here put an end to further talk; and a few minutes after Florence was going down to the dining-room with Mr. Stuart.

"You have just returned home, have you not?" she asked, to begin a conversation which she expected, from what she could judge from the gravity of his expression, would not be of the most lively.

"Yes; I came from London three days ago."

"I suppose it is very dull at this time of year."

"London is never dull; at least, not to me; but, then, I suppose the place where a man's work is, must always be the most interesting to him. The same as her home is never dull to a woman."

"I am afraid the correctness of that last generalization, at least, might be disputed."

"Yes, I suppose I was wrong, or we should not have so many women who seek relief from ennui in the pleasures of society. I have myself met so few of these, and so thoroughly believe in the home-loving, home-keeping woman being the true type of her sex, that, for the moment, I had forgotten their existence."

"There are many women who find the greatest pleasure in mixing in society, and to whom the exclusiveness of an entirely domestic life would be very irksome. A man is not supposed to be satisfied with merely domestic interests, and I do not see why a woman should, who by nature is even more socially inclined."

"Have you got on that weighty subject— the comparative merits of the two sexes— Miss Florence? Pray speak louder, that we

may have the benefit of your observations.
Mrs. Aylmer, may I beg that you will call for
silence? Miss Florence Aylmer is going to
be kind enough to speak to us."   .

Mr. Carrick, a cousin of Mr. Aylmer's,
who was often in the house, and who said this,
was seated opposite Florence, and had been
listening to her for some time. Notwithstanding some disadvantages of personal
appearance, his quiet self-possession and composure under all circumstances, and the
consideration with which he expressed himself, did not fail to carry weight.

"It only is, mamma, that Mr. Carrick wants
there to be silence, that he may be heard
talking," said Florence, when appealed to.

"We are waiting to hear you talk, Mr.
Carrick, now that you have silenced us," said
a Miss Cadogan.

"Really, Mrs. Aylmer, I feel so distressed,
you can't think, that I should have caused

Miss Cadogan to be silent. I know what a restriction it must be. Pray, beg her to speak on, since Miss Florence Aylmer will not give us the benefit of her learning, after all."

" You think I like talking?" asked Miss Cadogan.

" I know you do," he replied, laughing a little.

"You are interrupting general conversation, Mr. Carrick; so I beg you will either be silent, or confine your attention to your next neighbour," said Mrs. Aylmer.

" But, when my next neighbour will have none of my attention, it is rather hard. Miss Scott, do you hear? Mrs. Aylmer says you are to attend to me, and not to Captain Legrand. It is all Mr. Aylmer's fault, that we have gone wrong, for talking to his left-hand neighbour."

After this interlude, general conversation began again. But Florence, for one, felt the second beginning more difficult than the first.

" Does your sister Anne still attend the lectures on Comparative Philology this year?" she asked.

" No; I am glad to say, she has given them up.   She had no time—her other work was much more important."

" Do you think so ?   Do you not think that the cultivation of a talent must always be important ? "

" I do not see of what importance a more thorough knowledge of Comparative Philology could be to her; but, at any rate, the value of her other work was such as far to outweigh any it might have."

" I do admire, so intensely, anyone who gives up their life, as she does, to the doing of good works.   And I suppose it would spoil the entirety of her life if the sacrifice were less complete.   But, still, every one does

owe something to himself, and self-cultivation
is an end in itself."

" Self-cultivation ? Well, but is the cultivation of our moral or our mental capabilities the more important ? It can hardly
be a question, it seems to me."

" But a man whose moral capacities alone
are cultivated, would be very one-sided and
exclusive."

" We have not time to be anything but
one-sided. We must work, or we must
think. Thought makes men anxious to see
and search further before they act, and so
puts an end to action, or makes it undecided,
hesitating, and useless. My sister, some
years ago, gave herself up to self-cultivation,
and finally got completely entangled in a
web of doubts and difficulties. She threw
it aside at last, and saved herself by
action."

" But thought, though it does not lead to

direct action, is an action itself which in-
fluences life. The men of thought help the
men of action; they give the light by which
the others must walk. I do not say the
one is better than the other; but only that
both are necessary."

"They do not give light; they turn us
aside into the ways of darkness," he replied,
gravely.

"Who does that? What dreadful people
are you talking of, Miss Aylmer?" demanded
Miss Cadogan.

"It is a long story," replied Florence,
smiling.

"But I want to hear about these dreadful
people. I feel quite curious. May I not
hear about them?"

"Don't let us talk about any dreadful
people, but come away to the drawing-
room," said Mrs. Aylmer; and the ladies
rose.

"Well, Florence, what of the curate?"
asked her mother.

"He thinks the plan by which the uni-
verse was made, was—heavens!—'was his
small nine-and-thirty articles.' He has his
sisters' intolerance quadrupled."

"Well, intolerance must be rather pleasant
for a variety," laughed Miss Cadogan. "Sure,
an' I likes a fariety; you are all free-thinkers
here. And, besides, he's so handsome, it
would be worth while coming out to dinner
to look at him. Mrs. Aylmer, whenever
you have Mr. Stuart, will you invite me?"

Miss Cadogan went up then to Anne
Stuart.

"Are you going to Mrs. Carrick's dance,
to-morrow?" she asked.

"No; we none of us go to balls, now."

"But this is a dance. It is not a ball at
all. It is quite innocent, I assure you."

"I do not doubt its innocence. I should

have said, I suppose, that we do not dance."

" Don't care about it ? Oh, by the bye, Mrs. Aylmer, did you hear Mrs. Carrick asked Mrs. Forbes to bring her daughter, and she answered, that she did not allow her to dance, for spiritual reasons ? Do you know if it is more spiritual to walk straight than round ? I wish you would tell me. I should like so much to be spiritual."

Hester Stuart laughed, but said more gravely—

" It is not the turning round Mrs. Forbes objects to; but the waste of time and force."

" You don't think it wrong, Miss Stuart?"

" No, not wrong. Wrong is a strong word."

" You only think it foolish ? You don't dance, either, Miss Florence Aylmer; is it for the same reason ?"

" No, Florence is too stately to care about rapid movement," said Hester, smiling.

> " A fair and stately maid, whose eyes
> Have touched the colour of the skies."

laughed Miss Cadogan.

When the gentlemen came up stairs, Mrs. Aylmer took an opportunity of introducing Mr. Stuart to Miss Cadogan, who made up her mind to draw out his intolerance.

" We have been discussing dancing," she said.

" Dancing ?   That must have been interesting and profitable ! " he said, drily.

" Yes, it was.   You know we have a great deal of dancing at this time of year. Do you think deux-temps or trois-temps is best ?"

" I never dance, so cannot offer an opinion."

" You don't dance ?   You should get M. D'Alvrecht to give you lessons; he is in

town at present. You and Mr. Carrick
should take lessons together."

" What is that about Mr. Carrick ?" asked
Mr. Carrick, turning round.

" Mr. Carrick ? There's nothing about
him, that I can see," she said, laughing.

" You were talking of me, I am convinced.
Miss Aylmer, did you not hear them talking
of me ?"

" Mr. Stuart is going to get dancing
lessons, and I proposed he should take you
with him. It would be an act of charity to
your partners."

" If Miss Cadogan will be dancing mistress,
I shall be delighted."

" Come away, and sing, Miss Cadogan,"
said Mrs. Aylmer.

" Now, Miss Cadogan," said Mr. Carrick,
following her to the piano, and speaking in
tones of remonstrance. " Do not sing love
songs. They are so absurd; and really, I

think, you are too sensible. You should not sing them."

She seated herself on the piano-stool, and, leaning forward, said impressively—

> " One word is too often disdained
>> For thee to disdain it."

" And," he replied,

> " One word is too often profaned
>> For thee to profane it."

" I did not know you studied Shelley."

"I am not so utterly ignorant, Miss Cadogan, as you seem to imagine, of the literature of my country."

" Shall I sing German, then ?"

"I don't like anything German," he said positively, but half laughingly.

" French, then ?"

"I don't like French, either. But why not sing English? It is a much finer language, and, I am sure, much more generally understood."

She sang,

> "My love is like a red, red rose."

"I regret you would not take my advice," he said.

"I believe love must be a painful subject with you just now, Mr. Carrick. I wish I had sung—

> "Life is real, life is earnest
> And this world is not its goal,"

—or,

> "There was a reaper, and his name was Death."

CHAPTER III.

" So hot a speed, with such advice disposed,
*   Such temperate order in so fierce a course,*
Doth want example."—SHAKSPERE.

" Serene and manly, hardened to sustain
*   The load of life."*—DRYDEN.

IT had been no hasty, ill-considered action on Ernest Stuart's part, to enter the Church; but the result of his whole education and character.

He had not been seized by any ardent, youthful enthusiasm, but had determined on the step gravely and sadly enough. Ambition, interest, and the advice of friends, had all pointed to a·more brilliant career, in which he felt he had power to win success, whilst the Church, he knew, only offered

him long years of hard, and probably thankless labour.

But he saw the world "half blind with
intellectual light, half brutalized with civilization, and mad with sin and pain," and
considered that the first duty of every man
was to find what physic he could for the
evil, and that a life would be well spent,
which had served to mitigate the lot of even
a few individuals here.

Mitigation was all he hoped and laboured
for; so that if there was little ardent enthusiasm, there was a great measure of
self-devotion. He did not suppose that a
clergyman alone is able to benefit his race,
and knew that a man may be equally useful
in other professions—perhaps, having a wider
extent of influence, even more so. But then
he knew, on the other hand, that if he
entered another profession, the gratification
of his own ambition would become his

object in life. Florence Aylmer may have
been right when she spoke of him as intolerant. He had been educated in a bigoted
Calvinism, and had not yet freed himself
from his swaddling clothes, for, during the
three years he had had his curacy, he had
been so occupied in teaching and helping
others, that he had no time left to teach
himself. He had allowed his individuality
to be absorbed in his work, which work, it
is true, was often hindered and impeded by
his want of light; for not seeing his way
clearly, he as often wounded himself as
helped others. On the other hand, his
teaching appealed more forcibly to the uncultivated intellects with which he had to
deal, than it would have done had it been
more enlightened and refined.

He really believed that he "had not time
to be anything but one-sided." Life was
short—twenty-six years of his had gone

already—and there was work, necessary
work, on every side, and few, if any, to do
it. So far as he could see, cultivated men
did less of it than those who were uncultivated; because, having a certain amount
of light, they could not rest till they had
more. He could not understand how men
could speak of self-cultivation as an end in
itself, when there was a world groaning in
misery around them; and felt it more incumbent on him to work on with what
powers he had, and succeed in little, though
he might fail in much, than to spend his
life in seeking light.

He had taken a curacy in one of the
poorest districts in London, and devoted
himself, heart and soul, to his work. He
had begun, as I have said, with no ardent,
youthful enthusiasm, to be disappointed, but
with a firm and manly resolve to go on uninfluenced and unwearied, though he should

be met by constant failure, believing that in the end some sort of harvest must be reaped from seed carefully sown.

The worst effect of his intolerance was to have made him grave and stern, and to have taken all the brightness from his life. He could not have been human, had he been able to look with a smiling face on more than three-fourths of his fellows hastening to perdition, although it is true he had not yet realized the full force and significance of his own doctrines. Experience had many lessons in store for him, and to such men her lessons are always bitter.

Miss Cadogan had been right when she remarked on his good looks. He was tall, slight, and erect. He was never known to lounge or stoop, for he was a man whom nature would have to compel to give way entirely, before he would give way in the least. The hair which clustered round the

pale high forehead, as well as that of the
small moustache, whiskers, and short crisp
beard, was raven black. The large deep-set
hazel eyes glowed with suppressed enthusiasm; while the aquiline nose, strongly-
marked brows, and somewhat hard lines
about the well-cut mouth, gave the face a
character of stern decision. The complexion
was olive, and, though usually pale, would
occasionally flush under the influence of a
sudden thought.

Ernest was the eldest of the family, and
though the parents were both dead, his
three sisters and two brothers lived together
in their house in Sedgeborough, next the
Aylmers'. They had been educated in a
strong regard for family relations; and although they had grown to be men and
women, with most distinct individualities,
they were all on close terms of friendship.

Each in their different way overflowed

with energy and zeal. " These Stuarts," some one had said, "should be dealt over the country, so that energy may not be concentrated all in one focus."

They were unconscious of the immense superiority they possessed, and were utterly incapable of understanding or sympathizing with indolence. Their energy, moreover, never died away aimlessly for want of an object; for, wherever they might be, they always succeeded in finding work.

The sisters called themselves women, not girls; and took all the privileges of women. They never hesitated to go about alone, or to find their own employments and occupations; and what was conventionality, that it should bind them down?

It was very pretty and very proper for little girls not to go about the streets alone or to be in the house after a certain hour; but they would as soon have put on pinafores,

and gone back to the nursery and mud pies
as have been these little girls. They had
lived in Sedgeborough all their lives, but
were still a source of never failing amazement to their quiet and ordinary fellow
citizens, who treated them very much as
children would their toys, expecting that,
when a certain string was pulled, they would
go on being amusing for a given time; and,
if the machinery happened not to work quite
so well as usual, feeling as though their just
rights had been denied.

Hester ministered most to their amusement. She would sit down in a business-
like manner, and do her best to fulfil her
friends' expectations, thinking it odd enough
all the time to be made a show of. I can
see her now, with her feet crossed, her hands
clasped in her lap, and a curious smile curling
the corners of her mouth, as she consented,
on being " wound up," to exhibit her eccen-

tricities, for the entertainment of the spec-
tators.

To Hester the generality of Sedgeborough
people did great injustice. Her sense of the
ludicrous was so strong, that even on serious
subjects she could not resist expressing herself in the most comical manner; and this
struck strangers so forcibly, that they forgot
to notice the thoughtfulness that lay beneath.
They looked on her simply as some vague
amusing phenomenon, supposing that Anne
had absorbed all the depth of mental capa-
bility which nature had to spare for the
women of the family, and Cecil all the moral
and lovable qualities. Whilst, had they
really tried to understand Hester, they would
have found, beneath all her fun and gaiety,
a depth of thought and a readiness of sympathy of which they had no conception.
She considered herself very uncultivated,
and was constantly regretting " neglected

opportunities." " But it shall not be," she said at this time; "I must not be so disgracefully ignorant. I am going to turn over a new leaf and begin to work. It would have been so nice had I only had literary tastes."

Although she was only two and twenty, she would talk sadly enough of the present generation, as though she were not of it; for she felt that she belonged to a world that was gone, and could only look with astonishment, not unmixed with admiration, on the ways and manners of the day. This feeling may have been right in a measure. Her eager conservatism—her theories as to woman's position and woman's duties — her submission to and respect for her elders—her reverence for and her opinions on education— all belonged to an order that had passed away. She was idealistic in many ways, given to hero worship, and had a loyal and true heart.

In appearance she was striking, though she had certainly no actual prettiness about her. Her figure was tall and somewhat angular; her hair and colouring nondescript; her forehead broad, her eyes grey, and her mouth firm and sweet. As Anne had no inclination for housekeeping or domestic management, Hester took these duties on herself and fulfilled them with zeal. It was on her that her brothers Edward and Louis relied for their home comfort. These men, both lawyers by profession, lived in hopes of doing well some day; and, though that day still lay far off in the future, it was likely that, if perseverance and study bring success, they should be successful.

Edward was a grave, quiet man, who was accustomed to speak with a certain precision and determination, which there was no gainsaying. As he went on his way, he looked neither to the right nor the left, so that it seemed as

though he had fixed his prominent clear blue
eyes on some distant object from which nothing
would turn him aside. Of him his sister
Anne said: "He is a good fellow, and may
be relied on," for, notwithstanding the affection which existed between them all, they
never scrupled to discuss each other, for they
were unable to see why there should be any
hesitation felt in the outspeaking of a truth.

When Ernest and his sisters returned from
the Aylmers', Anne said,—

"The more I see of these people, the more
I am struck with their interest in life and all
its concerns. Their sympathies are open
and ready. Florence is coming with me to
Redfern Hospital to-morrow."

"Are you sure there is not more curiosity
to see the different forms of life, than sympathy with suffering?" asked Ernest.

"A little of both," said Hester, laughing.

"I often think they like to draw us out

for their amusement, but quite kindly! As Ernest says, it is just curiosity in the different forms of life."

" They ' do admire you so intensely,' but like studying you as curious phenomena."

" I think you do them great injustice," said Anne decidedly; " we have not such ready interest as they in all the different forms of life. We are very exclusive, and if we were to ' so admire' a little inexclusiveness, and to some purpose, it might do us good."

" There is danger in inexclusiveness, and in such admiration, wasting itself in simple admiration, instead of having result in action."

" I am aware there is danger which cannot be too strictly guarded against. I think, however, Mrs. Aylmer is most sensible, and will stop her daughters in time, if they become unsound in their judgment."

" And, as for acting, I rather like the idea

of there being pretty young creatures, who, without working themselves, encourage the workers with their sympathy."

"My dear Hester, I thought you would have been too sensible. Of course it would be very pleasant for the workers if there were 'pretty young creatures' whose sole object in life would be to sympathize with them. But what of the 'pretty young creatures'? It would hardly be for their advantage."

"It was something like Comte's proposal, that woman should be supported in enforced idleness by the community, in order to form an ideal of humanity," said Edward.

"Wait a moment, I have something," cried Hester, and then continued bringing out her words with pain and difficulty, but beaming with triumph when they were uttered. "'Nur das Händeln giebt dem Manne ein würdiges Dasein.'"

"Well done, Hester," said Ernest, laughing, as he laid his hand with affection on his sister's.

"The 'a' in 'Handeln' is long," said Anne, and, taking up her candlestick, went to her room.

CHAPTER IV.

"Here comes Beatrice : by the day, she's a fair lady.
I do spy some marks of love in her."—'MUCH ADO
ABOUT NOTHING.'

"*Ros.* How full of briars is this working-day world !
"*Cel.* They are but burs, cousin, thrown upon thee in
holiday foolery.   If we walk not in the trodden paths, our
very petticoats will catch them."—'AS YOU LIKE IT.'

BEATRICE CADOGAN was the only child of ·
Theophilus Cadogan and Sophia his wife.
Mr. Cadogan, as his daughter would have
everyone remember, was the second son of
Sir Peter Cadogan, of Cadogan.   It was
such a comfort, Beatrice said, to think that
she was even distantly connected with the
peerage; and, as for being poor, what was
that ! Poverty was so " genteel." It was
quite a title to aristocracy in itself.   She

looked down from the Olympian heights of three hundred pounds a year with pity on those plebeians who wallowed in their thousands, and, as for the unfashionable part of the town in which she lived, it was so quiet that she would have preferred it under any circumstances.

Beatrice had forgotten, most probably, that Sir Peter Cadogan had made his money by a stocking manufactory, this forgetfulness on her part being excusable, as Sir Peter had left all this, except the few thousands, from which the three hundred pounds were derived, to his eldest son, the present baronet. As for her great-grandfather, she had not a chance of remembering anything about him, as no one knew what he was, or from whence he had come. So it was that she talked of her proud lineage, and her aristocratic birth.

Moreover, as his descent was the only

thing remarkable about her father, it was incumbent on his dutiful daughter to respect that descent. When Mr. Cadogan had considered life, 'twas all a cheat, for he had lived in constant expectation of winning renown, and had always been on the point of writing a book, or making a discovery which was to give him at once a fortune, and a name. But some one was always before him, and wrote or discovered what he was going to write or discover, or the point slipped away from him as he was near its attainment. "My dear," his wife had said, " you had much better give it up, and let us lead a quiet life." But Mr. Cadogan had not given it up, notwithstanding all his wife's assurances that for him to attempt to do anything would be utterly futile; and, until he died, which happened some years before this story opens, he believed as firmly as ever in his own capabilities and chances of achievement.

Mrs. Cadogan had not meant to be unkind to her husband; but she had seen how vain would be all his endeavours, and so had wished to save himself and her from being discomposed.

"Papa keeps us in such a pleasant state of expectation," Miss Cadogan once said, "that we have not time to be dull; we are always hoping to be rich."

She was sixteen years of age when he died, and was now two-and-twenty, and so may have experienced several disappointments herself by this time. If she had, she had borne them with tranquillity and composure; but, then, it is true, that society expects women to bear their disappointments with composure; and, though Miss Cadogan was thoroughly self-reliant and independent, she did, in some things, recognize the power of conventionality.

Her uncle, Sir Peter Cadogan, was a

widower with three sons, which, in two ways, was a great satisfaction to Miss Cadogan.

Firstly: If he had had daughters, she would have ceased to be Miss Cadogan; and she felt she would not have borne with equanimity to have gone through life as Miss Trichy, which was the name by which she was familiarly known.

" This may appear trivial," she said ; "but life is made up of such trivialities, and hath it not been said, 'Despise not the day of small things' ? "

Secondly : When she went to Cadogan she could enjoy the superabundance of good things there much more at her ease than she could have done had there been a mistress of the household. She even preferred to pay her visit when none of her cousins were at home, for they were sandy-haired, troublesome young men, whose presence interfered with her comfort and freedom of action.

In their absence she would revel in the luxury around her much more thoroughly, for her uncle was very inobtrusive, and kept to his own study. She could therefore lounge idly in easy chairs and sofas, or read the newest book, as it suited her; could play on a splendid piano, or a still more splendid organ, as the humour struck her. She could occupy herself also, and this she considered very delightful, in arranging and re-arranging the furniture of the different rooms. And if all these pleasures should chance to pall, as pleasures will at times, she had only to send for Mrs. Budget, the housekeeper, who she knew could always give her entertainment, for housekeepers have so much experience of life, and know interesting things that no one else knows.

During these visits at Cadogan she considered that her virtue was put to a severe test, for she was constantly tempted to break

the sixth commandment. There were so
many things in the house which she would
have liked to possess, and that no one would
have missed. It was really quite a question
in casuistry. If she took the things she
would be benefiting her uncle, for it would
prevent him from being a dog in the manger
and keeping what had no value for him:
but then she would injure herself. Whether
should she do good to herself or to others?
Sir Peter Cadogan, she thought, might have
done more than open his doors to her, but
this seemed never to occur to him; and,
although he was gracious to his niece, he
never gave her any substantial help. One
reason for this may have been that his sister-
in-law was so little a favourite of his, that he
could hardly tolerate her presence in his
house. The baronet had many prejudices
and fancies which were treated with no consideration by his sister-in-law; moreover, she

had been a governess, and it was not surprising that his sense of the fitness of things
should be outraged at the idea of plebeian
blood mixing with that of the noble family
of Cadogan, of Cadogan ; for Sir Peter, as
well as his niece, had a conveniently short
memory on some matters. When he had
heard that his brother had really married, he
told his wife that he supposed they must ask
" the person" to pay them a short visit,
" for, as Mrs. Theophilus Cadogan, some
attention is due to her."

Mrs. Theophilus Cadogan — " Heavens!
that I should be called upon to go into
society with such a name," had been her
first exclamation on being led from the
altar. Mrs. Theophilus Cadogan, I say, had
taken from her husband all her brother-in-
law's letters with regard to his marriage,
and, reading them, made every word food for
laughter; and determined not to forget the

disparaging terms which had been applied
to her.

" I believe your grandfather may have
had a right to the first syllable of his name,
if you like,—to nothing else," she once said
to the irate baronet, when he had been talking to her about the duties she would have
to fulfil in her present position. " I shall
have many difficulties, you say? Of course
I shall. It will be very difficult to live on
three hundred a year, especially if we have
many children; and when people are poor
they have always a number of children."

On hearing these words the honourable
baronet's face flushed, his under jaw fell, and
his gold eye-glass dropped from the exquisite
balance in which it had been held between
his fingers. That a woman should talk thirteen or fourteen days after her marriage
about her future family and the probability
of its being large, appeared to him immodest,

indecent, inconceivable. As for Mrs. Theophilus Cadogan, she would have turned any hesitation to do so on her part to scorn. It was an undoubted fact that married women have children — a provision of nature, and therefore, why not speak of it? Those women ashamed of child-birth should devote themselves to a life of celibacy.

"How is it, Peter?" she asked,—for she had never given him his title, these sort of people are always familiar,—" how is it, Peter, that you have no portraits of your ancestors? I expected from your letters to your brother to find dark wainscoted walls lined with pictures. Where did your people live before your father bought this house?"

" They came over from Ireland."

" From Ireland? Dear me! all your ancestors? I am afraid you cannot have had many of them."

"If you would allow me to explain myself?"

She bowed.

" My father was Irish, and settled in this country."

" How was it that he lost his fortune ?— for he was a weaver, was he not ? I feel so interested."

" A—a weaver, Mrs. Theophilus Cadogan?"

" Would you oblige me by dropping the Theophilus,—as your wife is Lady Cadogan there can be no objection. Yes; a weaver; don't you understand ? One whose employ- ment is to work with a loom, as a dictionary would have it. Was that not his trade, or did your respectable mother support him by knitting stockings ? I have heard both stories."

After such a conversation as this it was natural enough that Sir Peter should avoid his sister-in-law, and wish to have her as little as possible in the house.

Miss Cadogan was more like her father in

personal appearance than her mother, and so
Sir Peter had been gracious to her. Her hair
was fair, but, as she said, the supply might
have been more plentiful. " The puffs, I
know, show behind when mamma does not
dress it carefully : if only I were rich, I should
supply the deficiencies of nature," she had
once remarked. But the forehead, which the
hair shaded, was broad and noble, while the
complexion of the oval face was delicate as a
sea-shell faintly tipped with pink. The short-
sighted prominent blue eyes were made to
appear even darker than they were in colour
by the dark yellow-brown lashes and brows.
The lips were thin, and closed firmly over
the slightly projecting white teeth. It was a
face which looked best in repose, and,
knowing this, she studied composure and
checked any vivacity of expression she might
have.

She was considered to have abilities above

the average, though she could not have passed an examination in any single branch of knowledge. " I went in for general ideas," she said, " as I found them the most easy and pleasant of attainment, and most useful in society. Women won't enter professions in my time, therefore I need not go through the drudgery of preparing for one."

If she was ignorant on any subject, she did not hesitate to confess the fact; then, probably the subject would be explained to her if it was one of general interest, which was, as she expressed it, " learning made easy."

She was musical, and enjoyed few things more than to spend a morning over a piano or an organ; yet she could not be called a performer, for though she entered into the spirit of the composition she rendered, she never played with perfect correctness.

" I am not a nervous young lady," she

said; " therefore I don't object to play in public. I don't want people to think me better than I am."

Beatrice had seen a good deal of life of one kind or another. Mrs. Theophilus Cadogan was an excellent manager of finances, and a most enterprising woman. She and her daughter were asked and went everywhere in Sedgeborough society, notwithstanding their limited wardrobes. In summer they went abroad and travelled about in the most extraordinary manner. They had been through Switzerland, France, and the North of Italy, and one year they had gone to Norway in a ship belonging to a Mr. Richardson, a cousin of Mrs. Cadogan. Mrs. Cadogan said she would prefer to starve a little to remaining in Sedgeborough all the year round. Also, she did not object to a few hardships, and her daughter would bear them with equanimity, which was, perhaps, as

well, as Mrs. Cadogan, when she wished
anything, was apt to say with Hudibras:

> " This must be done, and I would fain see
> Mortal so sturdy as to gainsay."

Mrs. Cadogan wished her daughter to marry.
" Why don't you marry," she said to her;
" don't you know you are growing old ? "
Beatrice's face flushed a little.

> " There is no one coming to marry me,
> There is no one coming to woo,"

was all she replied. Mrs. Cadogan believed
that Beatrice had her father's hopeful disposition, and would not marry those whom she
could, because she believed that she should
marry some one she could not. For Mrs.
Cadogan remembered how, two years ago,
when they were in Switzerland, they had
become acquainted with a Major Aylmer, a
nephew of Professor Aylmer, and how she
had hoped that he would become her daugh-

ter's husband : for the two had been much together, and, although they occasionally disagreed strongly, had seemed to get on more than well on the whole.

When the Cadogans continued their travels Major Aylmer had gone with them, arranging their journeys, and taking care that Miss Cadogan should have the best opportunity of seeing the scenery of the country.

This went on for some weeks, until at last they came to Lucerne.

One afternoon when there, Maurice Aylmer and Beatrice had gone out together, and some time later, when they returned, Beatrice hastened up to her room, and Major Aylmer went to tell Mrs. Cadogan that he had made up his mind to return to England immediately, having been away longer already than he had intended.

He left two days after, but during these two days the Cadogans saw little or nothing of him. He had a number of arrangements, he said, to make before his departure, and Mrs. Cadogan drily agreed that they seemed to be numerous.

It was for her daughter's own sake Mrs. Cadogan wished her to be married and settled. She was poor, with expensive tastes, and friendless, so that her future, as a single woman, would not be exactly paradisaical. Her mother had once said to her, " In making your arrangements, I hope you remember that when I am removed, in the course of nature, you will be alone in the world."

Mrs. Cadogan was, therefore, thoroughly disappointed. It must have been some foolish misunderstanding, and was particularly vexatious, as Major Aylmer appeared to be to her daughter's taste, as well as rich, handsome, and clever. If Beatrice were disappointed, she kept it to herself, for women do not show these things.

Major Aylmer had had an ideal of what a woman should be, and might have said, in the words of a song which Beatrice made him sing, "She must be holy, pure, and tender, my queen."

There was much that was womanly and gracious in Miss Cadogan's character; and this, combined with her talents and the charm of her manners, had fascinated him before he was aware. Her words had often jarred upon him and his sense of what should be, and he would show her his disapproval, from whence would follow those occasional disagreements which Mrs. Cadogan had noticed.

"Why should you not call a spade a spade?" she asked.

"There are some spades," was his answer, "which had better not be mentioned at all."

"You would have us women shut up like chimney ornaments, under glass cases; so that if any rumour of evil around us should reach us, we should put our taper fingers to our delicate ears, lisping. 'I don't believe it.'"

He replied, sternly,—

"When there is a keen sense of the evil, the matter is different, Miss Cadogan. It is the familiarity and almost enjoyment in the expression of it that is objectionable."

"You don't mince matters, Major Aylmer," she said, laughing.

When Major Aylmer became conscious of the extent of his feelings with regard to Miss Cadogan he was vexed, remembering how she differed from his ideal, that he should have allowed them to arise. For a moment he thought of conquering these feelings in the belief that a union between them could not be for the happiness of either; but then, again, he thought that if he could win her love, much that he disliked would be altered.

" If love is a power," he thought, " it will soften her, and she has not a weak character which must be at the command of the moment's impulse. She is strong enough, I believe, to conquer herself." He had, therefore, followed where she went, till they came to Lucerne.

When here, Miss Cadogan had outraged him in every way conceivable, and he had begun to doubt the wisdom of his resolution. During these days Miss Cadogan was under the influence of excitement, so that she hardly knew what she did, was " ausser sich," as the Germans would say.

Major Aylmer tried his power to restrain her, determining to judge thereby what his chances of success in the future might be ; but she proved restive, and he seemed to have none.

They went out for a walk one afternoon, and had sat down to admire the beauty of the view, and talk more at ease.

Then it was that Beatrice had said those
words which had separated her from Maurice
Aylmer. When he heard them, he had merely
said a stern " Miss Cadogan!" and there was
silence between them.

Intuitively she knew that this was the last
straw which had broken the horse's back.
Her excitement died within her, and she felt
faint and sick at heart, with all the enormity
of her sins lying heavily upon her.

He rose. " Shall we return?" he asked,
coldly.

She got up and walked silently back. At
any other time she would have shown peni-
tence in a thousand different ways, until she
had forced forgiveness. She was a very
woman, in so far that she could not bear to
live with people who disapproved of her;
but now she felt that all was at an end
between them; that Major Aylmer's determination was taken, and would not be

moved by any pretty penitences on her
part.

On returning to the house she went at
once to her own room. Seating herself, she
leant her elbow on a table, and her head on
her hand, and struggled against the feeling
of faintness that had come over her. She
could have cried for a little thing, such as
having over-fatigued herself, or the wind
being in the east, for which Aurora Leigh
says women only shed tears; but she could
not cry now. During the two days which
elapsed before Major Aylmer left Lucerne,
Beatrice felt that life was very bitter, and
not worth having. She had to smile, talk,
and look as usual; to fear both her mother's
and Major Aylmer's scrutiny.

Had Beatrice to live that summer month
in Switzerland over again, she would have
acted very differently, and the probability is
that she would have become Mrs. Aylmer.

She had grown wiser by this time; for, after
all, she had had the excuse of youth, and it
is rather hard that we should expect women
to be perfectly sensible, wise and discreet
at eighteen, when men are pardoned for
youthful wild oats to a much later date.

Had Beatrice not felt she had been to
blame, and had only herself to thank for
what had happened, I do not think that she
would have improved or grown wiser.

A woman is always gentle and considerate
of others till she has been taught, by experience, the hardness and inconsiderateness of
the world, and when men blame women for
their hardness and bitterness, saying that in
this is the cause of their loss of influence,
they might look nearer home to find of what
this again is the result.   As bitterness in a
man is generally caused by disappointed
idealism, of having expected to find the
world better than it is, so in a woman, it is

caused by disappointed trust, by having expected to find one person better than he is. A man talks to a woman, either openly of love, or in tones of love, and tries to make her return the same to him in kind, saying, in point of fact,—

> "Thus, when thou hast proved me, dear,
> Woman's love no fable,
> I will love thee half a year
> As a man is able."

And having loved his half year, he goes away and leaves her, and the next comer finds her bitter and hard in her words, and inconsiderate in her deeds.

Men are not affected in the same way, I suppose, as a rule, because their affections are wider; they are like limpets, which, when loosened from one rock by the invading sea, can find as great comfort and ease on another. If the human limpets are inclined to stay in the sea now, it may suit them to blame the rocks, but is it not really their own fault and loss? Who shall say?

When Beatrice had known Major Aylmer, she had been merely a foolish girl, who did not understand the full force of her words; and had he asked her to be his wife, I think he would have found that he had not made a mistake. She had not been really hard and careless of the opinions and feelings of others, and would have been incapable of flirting and playing with men for her own amusement.

Miss Cadogan was not broken-hearted by what had occurred, and did not immediately think fit to "languish in despair." She enjoyed life and its pleasures as much as ever, and much more fully than most women do, having an immense fund of enjoyment in herself, and great capabilities for making the best of that enjoyment. If she ever felt inclined to be sentimental, and ask "where is it now, the glory and the dream?" she would check herself, and, declaring it was bathos, would ask whether it was the result of over-fatigue or a better-dressed woman. Yet, notwithstanding this, she had nothing of the limpet in her nature, and because she could not marry Major Aylmer, did not transfer her affections to the most suitable who came in her way.

Mrs. Cadogan hoped that the friendship which now existed between her daughter and Mr. Carrick might ripen into something more. "And, after all, friendship is the best foundation for love and marriage," thought Mrs. Cadogan with a sigh, for she had been disappointed in the love in a cottage which she had chosen.

Beatrice knew well that it would never do for her to marry Mr. Carrick, for she could say what she liked to him without fearing any reproof he might give. She wished to be ruled, and the only thing which fate had given her, of which she was heartily sick, was liberty.

> "'Tis licence I have, when I have liberty,
> For who love that must first be good and wise,"

she said, adapting the words of the poet to suit her own convenience.

CHAPTER IV.

"Sound, thou trumpet of God; come forth, Great Cause,
   to array us!
King and leader appear, thy soldiers sorrowing seek
   thee!
Would that the armies, indeed, were arrayed.   O! where
   is the battle?
Neither battle I see, nor arraying, nor King in Israel.
Only infinite jumble, and mess, and dislocation,
Backed by a solemn appeal, 'For God's sake, do not stir
   there.'"   A. H. CLOUGH.

THE morning after the Stuarts had dined at
the Aylmers', Ernest was employing himself in finishing a drawing of his sister
Cecil's, when Anne looked in at the door.
It was ten o'clock, and having sat up late
at night, this was her first appearance, and
she was already cloaked and bonneted, ready
to go out.

"Cecil, are you to be in this afternoon?" she asked.

"No, I have a class at Brompton."

"Is Hester to be in?"

"Probably not; but I cannot answer for Hester's movements."

"That is wise, for they are slightly erratic," said Ernest, smiling.

"Well, then, Ernest, Florence Aylmer is to be here at half-past two, to go to Redfern Hospital; and if I am not in then, you must bring her to Redfern Lane, and I shall meet you there."

"And what will Miss Florence Aylmer say to being left to my care instead of that of my discreet sister?"

"You won't eat her, I suppose. It is better that Miss Florence Aylmer should take half-an-hour's walk with you, than that work should be neglected. I shall try to be home, but am afraid it will be useless."

"Don't try, then, Anne. It is certainly better Miss Aylmer should have half-an-hour's walk with me, than that you should be over-worked."

"And clean up your paints, Cecil, when you are done," said Anne; "and tidy the room." With which she left, and might shortly after have been seen hastening down the street, looking neither to the right nor the left,—people giving way before her, notwithstanding her slight, fragile appearance.

"Neat," said Cecil, "Anne asking Florence Aylmer to walk with her, and then going off in this way. Mrs. Aylmer will hardly approve."

Florence was surprised, when asking at the door for Miss Stuart, to hear the servant say something about "Mr. Ernest." But supposing it to be a mistake, she followed her in.

Ernest met her in the hall. "My sister

was obliged to go off on some of her work," he said, in a quiet, matter-of-fact way. " And as I am the only idle one of the family, she has instituted me her representative, to take you to Redfern Lane."

" And Miss Stuart?" asked Florence, in much hesitation.

" Will join us there," he answered. " Suppose we start at once. That is to say," he continued, noticing her hesitation, and smiling, " unless you are afraid of trusting yourself to me. I assure you the dangers of the street are few; and against such as there may be, I shall form a more efficient protector than my sister."

Florence hastily came to the conclusion that it would be wise to treat the affair as though it were the most natural that could have arisen, although, at the same time, she could not help thinking that the Stuarts were even more unlike other people than she had supposed. Ernest had spoken of its being half-an-hour's walk to Redfern Lane, but Florence knew that it would be really much longer, as the Stuarts might be counted on to walk at double the pace of other people. Moreover, she knew that she would have to pass through Edward and King Streets, and would probably meet friends who would not be a little surprised to see her walking with Ernest Stuart.

A sudden idea struck her as she went out of the house. " Did you notice Miss Frost at our house last night?" she asked, blushing, and stammering slightly. "I am sure she would like to come with us if she might. May I call at our house and see if she is in?"

Ernest acquiesced, but felt a certain contempt for a woman who could make a fuss about so small a matter as this. Florence rang, and inquired if Miss Frost were in?

"Out." " Miss Lois ?" she asked, in despair. Miss Lois was out with Miss Frost.

The fates were against her, without a doubt; for she had never known Miss Frost and Lois to be out at this time before. Ernest smiled when he heard the result of her attempt. " You will have to trust your-self to my care, after all," he said.

" Have you ever been at Redfern Hospital before ?" he asked, after a pause.

" Yes, I have been once or twice. I like going, particularly with Miss Stuart, for all the people seem to be so much at their ease with her."

" Why do you like to go ?."

" I never thought of putting the question to myself," she said, and smiled one of her rare sweet smiles. " It is partly, I suppose, because I like to see the people, and hear them talk. There is always a certain interest in seeing the different phases of life, I think."

"So you go to the hospital to study character," and there was the slightest shade of sarcasm in his voice.

"If you like to put it in that way; but it is rather unjust, for it appears as though I had no sympathy for the people, and placed myself on an eminence above them, while really I go to learn from them. They have all seen much more of life than I."

As he heard these words, he felt rebuked.

She went to learn where he would have gone to teach. Which was the more gentle and humble spirit? It could hardly be a question.

"Moreover," she continued, and smiled again, "they like our visits. They seem to brighten their lives; and I shall be candid enough to confess that it is pleasant to know that I have done some little thing for them in their sufferings."

"Does it not rather make you remember

how much lies in our power, and how little
we do?"

"I know that you mean that I should
work among the people, as your sisters do.
But you must remember that there are few
women who are free to choose their occupation, as your sisters are. I confess, however,
that probably, were I free to choose, I should
not decide on the course you seem to think
best."

At this moment they turned into Edward
Street, and came face to face with Mr. Carrick.
He took off his hat.

"I hope you are having a pleasant walk,
Miss Florence Aylmer," he said. "Is Mrs.
Aylmer here?" looking round inquiringly.

"No, mamma is not here. We are going
to Redfern Hospital. Miss Stuart and I
arranged it yesterday."

And Florence felt her explanation was very
lame, and was glad when Mr. Carrick asked,

—"Miss Stuart? Ah! is she here?" for it gave her an opportunity of mentioning that they were on their way to meet Miss Stuart.

"I shall beg my sister to make arrangements to walk with you too some day, Miss Aylmer," he went on. "But I see Mr. Stuart is anxious to go on. I shan't detain you longer. If I see Mrs. Aylmer, I shall mention that I have had the pleasure of meeting you," and, laughing a little, Mr. Carrick passed on.

Florence got more and more uncomfortable as she passed Mrs. Murray, whose little daughters went nowhere without their mother,—Mrs. Athole, whose daughters never walked two steps without a footman at their heels,—Sir Charles Richards, whose daughters were hardly allowed to say more than two words to any man,—Mr. Evans, whose daughter, Mrs. Aylmer openly said, was "really too fast,"—Captain Legrand, Mr.

Farebrother, and Mr. Willoughby. The whole of Sedgeborough seemed to have turned out that day, and Florence felt its curious eyes were on her.

It was a relief, at any rate, to know that Mr. Stuart was quite unconscious of any cause of annoyance on her part; and, moreover, that few people knew who he was; and, as a forlorn hope, the idea came to her that he might be thought a cousin.

Now they had left Edward Street, and had only a short way to go in King Street, and then they would get into a quiet, unfrequented part of the town. Florence also was convinced she had met everybody whom it was possible to meet.

" How do you do, Florence ? Do you not remember me?" said a well-known voice, just as she thought all danger was over; and Mrs. Cadogan and Beatrice stopped to speak to her.

"I did not see you," said Florence, blushing.

"Yes; you seemed absorbed! I doubted whether I should interrupt you or not. How do you do, Mr. Aylmer?" she continued, putting up her eye-glass. "It is a long—oh! I beg your pardon; I thought it was Mr. Aylmer with his daughter."

Florence introduced Mr. Stuart, and then began her explanations. again about Miss Stuart and the Redfern Hospital.

"I hope you will enjoy your walk," said Mrs. Cadogan; "it is certainly a fine day." And then they passed on, Florence pleasantly conscious that Mrs. Cadogan thought her walking about the streets with Mr. Stuart a very extraordinary proceeding. She did not care much whom she might meet after this.

Redfern Lane was soon reached now, where Anne Stuart joined them.

The hospital had been erected for the re-

ception of those whose illness was pronounced
incurable, and in it now were to be found a
curious collection of men and women of all
ages and occupations. It might be supposed
to be a sad and dreary enough place, as all
who were in it knew they would only leave
it to make their last journey; but they did
not seem, as a rule, oppressed by the sense
of the death which was approaching them;
and there was still to be found among them
a lively interest in the world and its concerns.
They were as ready to make eager friend-
ships or bitter enmities as though a whole
life lay before them, and were full of complaints as to the food and provisions of the
hospital. Into Anne Stuart's ears long stories
were poured by patients and nurses, with a
"But, wumman," or a "Do ye see, wumman";
and she had to be arbiter in many a quarrel.

Her interest in the hospital had first been
excited some years ago, when there had been

much sickness in the town, and its nurses had been drawn away to other institutions by the high salaries offered, so that the staff had become so small as to be totally inefficient for its work. Anne had then come forward, and had stayed for several months in the hospital as a regular nurse, shirking none of the labour and none of the inferior duties incumbent on her position. To all inquiries she would briefly reply, " She had liked it. It had been pleasant to get off her fine clothes, and physical labour was a relaxation to her." The lessons she had learnt during three months had been of the greatest service in her after-life. She could understand the feelings and characters of the people much more fully from having worked among them as one of themselves. She did not hesitate now to give active, substantial assistance, and might have been seen with her sleeves tucked up, and an apron tied on in front, scrubbing floors or clothes in many a house, whilst, in a case of sickness, her practical knowledge of the art of nursing was invaluable.

Florence had been, as she had said fairly, often at the hospital, and Ernest noticed with surprise that she seemed to be quite at home, and would talk to the people with a certain tact and good feeling which won their hearts. He was surprised, because he had looked on her as a beautiful statuette, only "sublime in great houses," and utterly incapable when confronted with real life, the life of the million. He had expected to see her, notwithstanding what she said about going to the hospital to learn, patronize those who had probably much more wisdom than she, simply in right of her purple and fine linen. As he watched her, he saw how faces brightened at her approach, and voices lost the asperity of their tones when addressing her; and he recognized that beauty and culture are powers, and not alone of the drawing-room.

"Live and learn," he thought, and unconsciously had learnt a great and important truth, his ignorance of which had made him impervious to many of the teachings of experience. He would have admitted before, of course, that in living he had to learn, but he had never realized the truth of this so clearly before.

He had been taught now that his judgment had been, in a measure, unjust, and this was at least one step in the right direction. He could not help observing the difference between his sister's and Florence's mode of action. The people did not hesitate to show Anne the worst as well as the better parts of their characters. No angry words and bitter complaints were softened to meet her ears,

and in return she did not scruple to blame
them roundly when occasion required, and
would make no reserve in telling them exactly what she thought of their conduct. To
her mind, an action was wrong or not wrong,
and an excuse was weak and contemptible.
This was a striking feature of her character,
and was the result of the same quality which
made her, whenever she spoke, avoid all
adjectives or paraphrases. A thing was
or it was not, and was to be stated in the
shortest words available. She would have
said that she had not breath to waste on
rounding her periods; and, indeed, her fair
pale face and slight gliding figure showed
that she had not strength of any kind to
waste.

When Florence Aylmer returned home,
she went to her own room, and drawing a
low chair to the fire, sat buried in thought,
though she had a book on her knee.

It had been curious to her to meet a man like Mr. Stuart, who despised all that she had been taught to respect, who thought that the attainment of intellectual light and culture was not an object of life. There had seemed to her to be so much confusion in the world, for all men were vaguely looking for a leader somewhere in the darkness, and, finding none, were rushing blindly on in their own way, too often increasing the misery around by their actions. The method and order of things were turned from their old way, and all creation appeared to cry out, " For God's sake, do not, stir there!" to those who would in their blindness physic the evil with quack remedies, which, after the first moment, served only to increase the weakness of the system. Florence laughed a little as she drew her picture home, and saw Ernest Stuart pouring black draughts down submissive throats. But though she

laughed, she believed the matter to be serious
enough.   "It were better," she thought,
"not to teach until he had something more
to teach than the distorted truths which are
all we possess.   But his actual work does
good, though his teaching may not."

CHAPTER VI.

"I come to visit thee in masquerade."—DRYDEN.

"Rattling nonsense in full volleys break."—POPE.

"Let order die."—SHAKESPERE.

FLORENCE had not much opportunity of telling her mother about her misfortunes that afternoon, as all such subjects were avoided before her father, and immediately after dinner they had to prepare for Mrs. Carrick's dance.

"It was unfortunate," Mrs. Aylmer said; " but Florence was not to blame; and every one knew that the Stuarts had an original way of arranging matters."

"You will get the credit of being a fast young lady, Florence, as well as an appallingly intellectual person," laughed Lizzie.

"And people will shake their heads," went on Lois, "saying they had always been convinced that poor dear Mrs. Aylmer would have to reap the fruits of having educated her family so ill, and they were sure they had constantly said so."

"Mr. Evans will ask Mrs. Forbes, 'If she has done this publicly, what must she not have done under the rose?'" added Lizzie.

"It is dreadful the freedom allowed to girls! I wonder what the world is coming to!" said Lois, in exact imitation of Mrs. Forbes's look and manner.

Florence went to Mrs. Carrick's because dances of the sort were always amusing to on-lookers, and she would join, too, in an occasional square dance.

When the Aylmers entered the Carricks' drawing-room, they found a large party already assembled. The guests were, however, all of the Aylmers' particular set, and

were exceedingly intimate among themselves.

Shortly after supper, Mrs. Cadogan came
and seated herself by Mrs. Aylmer.

" I did not know," she said, "that you
went in for the emancipation of young
ladies."

" It depends on what you mean by the
phrase."

" I do not mean emancipation from their
medical or political, but from their social
and conventional disabilities. And you
support your theory by practice, I see."

" Emancipation from social and conventional disabilities? I really wish I understood. In the first place, I do not see how I
could support any theory about a young lady
by practice; and, in the second, I consider
conventionality necessary, if tiresome."

" Oh, so your practice is more advanced
than your theory!"

"Now, Mrs. Cadogan, I demand an explanation," said Mrs. Aylmer, laughing; "for this really gets serious."

"Perhaps you think it is only an old-fashioned prejudice on our parts, to suppose that young ladies—I beg your pardon, young women, I know it is not the thing to speak of 'ladies' now-a-days, when we are all made after one fashion, with no difference in the quality—well! as I said, I suppose it is an old-fashioned prejudice that young women should not choose their own companions as well as young men. We are old-fashioned, I know, but confess I was not aware how far advanced you are. Do you go with Lizzie to the assembly on Wednesday, or does she go with Mr. Arbuthnot?"

Lizzie was at that moment dancing with a Mr. Arbuthnot, who was supposed to pay her great attention.

Mrs. Aylmer laughed, but looked vexed.

" Florence explained the circumstance of her walk with Mr. Stuart to you. What could the poor child have done ? I am sure I should not have known how to get out of the difficulty myself."

" Indeed! But then I do not think that even the strictest martinet could object to your walking with the young man, if you wished to do so."

" What are you discussing here ?" asked Mr. Aylmer, joining them.

" The propriety, or impropriety, of your wife taking a walk with Mr. Stuart."

" Ernest Stuart, the curate, do you mean? You must have small matter for discussion, if you can find much to say about that."

" I should certainly have supposed it to be quite an innocent amusement; but your wife seems to think she might experience some difficulty to avoid it."

"You have made a great deal out of my poor words."

"He's very handsome, I hear," went on Mrs. Cadogan, meditatively.

"Your daughter thought him so," burst in Mrs. Aylmer. But the other continued, paying her no heed, "Still, he is so young, I should not have thought there would have been any danger."

There was a cry at that moment that Mr. Carrick had disappeared, that he was not going to dance, and that it was shameful. A raid was made from the room of young men in search of the culprit. Mr. Carrick walked in at last, looking very like a lamb being led to the sacrifice, his persecutors following him in triumph. When called upon to explain his conduct, he, standing in the middle of the room, addressed the company in plaintive accents :—"A young lady, I shall not mention names," but his eyes rested on Miss Cadogan, "a young lady, at present amongst you, has, on another occasion, accused me of dancing badly, and expressed compassion for my partners. I have no desire to cause unhappiness to any young lady, particularly when she is a guest of my mother's. I therefore determined not to dance. May I retire? I wish to retire. Pray allow me."

There was a cry that Miss Cadogan must dance with him; and Beatrice came forward, bowed, made a step backwards, and bowed again, letting her hands hang loosely before her.

"Miss Carrick," he said, "will you do me the honour of taking a turn in the mazy?"

A waltz was struck up, and she said again, as they were dancing,—

"I did not know your nature was so tenderly sensitive."

"And why should I not have a sensitive nature, Miss Cadogan?"

"Oh! if you like it, there is no reason why you should not have it! I should have thought it would be a great inconvenience. Is it not?"

"I can't talk when waltzing, Miss Cadogan, really I can't. It is too much to expect."

"Are you giddy? I'll get you a chair. But if you won't dance with me, I shall dance with myself;" and, drawing her arm from his, she went on waltzing in the most graceful manner, and with the most perfect self-possession conceivable.

Mr. Carrick, thus left in the lurch, appealed to Florence, who sat near.

"Miss Florence Aylmer, pray look at Miss Cadogan. Is it customary for young ladies to dance by themselves? But really, now, is it customary?"

"If he won't waltz with you, let me," said

Mr. Arbuthnot, and would have claimed Beatrice, but Mr. Carrick came forward again.

" La, la, la," sang she, in tune to the music, and waltzed on equably, leaving them to their dispute. Mr. Rallis, an excitable old man, with long white hair, and a face that a painter would have coveted as a model, might have been seen, at this juncture, throwing himself on his knees before Mrs. Aylmer, kissing her gloved hand, and conjuring her to give him " one turn, for the love of heaven!"

" There might be some question as to propriety here," quoth Mrs. Cadogan. Florence and a Mr. Handbarn, to whom she was talking, were the quietest persons in the room. Mr. Handbarn had, at one time of his life, been the representative in Parliament of a large county; but now times were changed for him, and he was glad to accept

of any invitation to eke out a scanty subsist-
ence. He was well read, and could talk,
and talk well, on most literary subjects,
delighting in making long quotations from
classical poetry, and in showing his knowledge of out-of-the-way events or ancient
documents. His clothes, that might have
been robbed from a scarecrow, his long,
untidy beard, and general dishevelled appearance, would have induced a stranger,
who met him on the road, to take him for a
common vagrant.

The tumult in the room seemed to increase
with every moment, for the cotillion was
going on, and new and extraordinary figures
were being invented by ingenious minds.

Mrs. Aylmer turned with a laugh to
Captain Legrand, the only stranger in the
room.

" I hope," she said, " you do not think we
are often like this ? "

He smiled excusingly.

"Ah!" he replied; "I assure you I quite understand it is Sedgeborough."

"But that is exactly what you are not to think it is."

"I quite understand, I assure you."

And Mrs. Aylmer, with a sigh, gave up trying to say anything more. It did not matter much, she thought, what he might please to think of Sedgeborough manners; and she turned away to laugh at Mr. Carrick and Mr. Arbuthnot waltzing together with much spirit, having been rejected as partners by all the ladies.

CHAPTER VII.

" Anxious cares the pensive nymph oppressed."
" I 'll get me to some place more void."

SHAKESPERE.

" You have not opened your mouth for one hour, Trichy—for one hour and three minutes."

" And how many seconds, mamma?"

" One. I have been looking at the clock."

" A profitable employment!"

" I do not mean that I have been gaping at it all this time."

" Gaping would not have helped you much towards seeing."

" Oh, very well! if you will have a minute description. At three o'clock, when you yawned, I looked at the time; and again, when you last yawned, I looked, and found it to be precisely four minutes and one second after four o'clock. What have you been thinking of all this time, may I inquire?"

Miss Cadogan clasped her hands behind her head, and, stifling a yawn, said, " I have been meditating offering a visit to the worthy baronet."

" And what's that for?"

" A little change."

"What, are you pining away and becoming interesting?— are you suffering from any secret pain? Confide in me, and do not let concealment, like a worm in the bud, gnaw at your damask cheek."

" It's only a headache, mamma."

" That's no secret pain, at any rate. I have heard of nothing else the whole day."

" Seriously, I want to go to Cadogan, and get away for a little. My own idea of myself, my idea of other people's idea of me, and other people's real ideas, have been haunting me, as the witches haunted Macbeth."

Mrs. Cadogan cast up her eyes—" How affecting!"

" They have made me do things I should never have dreamt of doing."

" I am sure I am glad to hear that you have not dreamt of some of the things you have done. Such nightmare could only have been promoted by severe indigestion."

" I want to walk over ploughed fields study the crops, and entertain honest county big-wigs. A country gentleman is a most refreshing—"

" Notice in the *Lancet*. A new tonic discovered. Dr. Cadogan has, by one of his valuable experiments, found out that a country gentleman is an excellent tonic. This venerated physician, with his usual sacrifice of self where the welfare of his race is concerned, tried the effect of the tonic first on

himself, and found his shattered nervous
system instantly remedied. We can but express the gratitude all men must feel towards
him, wishing, at the same time, he would not
be so careless of his most valuable life. This
last experiment was quite foolhardy."

Beatrice continued :—

" The learned Dr. Cadogan had tried this
tonic some years previously, but his consti-
tution proved to be too fragile."

" So that," burst in her mother, " he
hardly survived the experiment."

" He therefore believes, to this day, that
the fault was in the tonic which really was
in himself. He forgets the old saying, ' Milk
for babes, but strong meat for men.' "

" You are too clever, Trichy ! Well ! so
you are going to be refreshed by county big-
wigs. When did you come to this conclusion ?"

Beatrice laughed.

" This morning, mamma, when I saw how
my pink silk had been destroyed by last
night's performances."

" Your dress will hardly be refreshed by
the ploughed fields ; at least, I should suppose not. If really they are good for dresses,
I shall send my black silk with you."

" Well ! shall I write to Sir Peter ?"

" Do anything you like, my dear."

Miss Cadogan rose, and went to the writing-
table. " Are there any stamps ?" she asked.

" There was a stamp left over yesterday.
But you speak of stamps ?   Perhaps a note
to a baronet requires more than one.   I have
not so much experience in matters relating to
baronets as a Cadogan by birth must have."

" Yes, there's a stamp."

Beatrice leisurely took the stopper from
the ink-bottle; then, resting her head on her
hand, remained staring out at the window.

" Out of the day and night
    A joy has taken flight,
    Fresh spring and summer and winter hoar
    Move my faint heart with grief, but with delight
    No more; oh, never more !"

quoted Mrs. Cadogan, in lugubrious accents.

" You must have a more obliging disposition, mamma, than I gave you credit for,
if winter hoar ever could have moved you to
delight," said her daughter, with a shudder.

Beatrice ·really did like the society she
met at her uncle's, and took an interest
in agricultural matters. She prided herself
on being a good judge as to the ploughing
of a field or the growth of a crop. She was
quite interested in potatoes and turnips, and
she thought people very well occupied who
were employed in their cultivation. They
were much more profitable, she was sure,
than ideas or theories, and she only wished
her father had recognized this : it would
have been better for himself and his family.

I think at times that she even persuaded
herself that she was made for a country life,
and was a farm-mistress spoiled. The case
really was, that everything with relation to
life interested her, and it was not merely for
an occupation, or in order to make herself
popular, that made her inquire into the feed-
ing and rearing of poultry, or made her take
the plough in her own slender hands, and
endeavour to make a straight furrow. She
had one disadvantage in all this : she was
not brave; and the sight of the most innocent of cows filled her with puerile fears.
One of her sandy-haired cousins had once
attempted to teach her to ride, but without
success.

"Is there any satisfaction," she asked,
"in being bumped up and down on the
back of a terrible animal like this?" And
then, again, "I suppose it will become pleasanter in time?"

But, although her cousin had endeavoured to persuade her that it would become pleasanter, Beatrice never trusted her person again on horseback.

"I think every sane person," she said, "is born with an instinct of self-preservation. I know, at any rate, that I have no desire to have my precious head broken. If I wished to put an end to my existence, I should choose a more agreeable method. Hamlet's bare bodkin, unpleasant as it sounds, would make a much better quietus."

"Oh! if you are going to quote poetry, I shall go!" said the sandy-haired cousin, which made Beatrice inclined to quote all the poetry she knew.

There was silence between Beatrice and her mother, and the ticking of the little brass clock on the mantelpiece made itself distinctly heard.

It is said that a room tells of the character

of its inhabitants; but this room of the Cadogans was merely suggestive of their poverty. It is only rich people who can afford to show their character in their furniture. The room was small, and ill lighted by two rather dusty windows.

"Let us be clean, whatever we are!" Beatrice had once exclaimed; and seizing her duster with her own fair hands, had rubbed hastily at the panes, and thought it rather an amusing employment.

"Cleanliness is next to godliness," she said, and rubbed again. But she soon grew tired of this, for there was no one to admire her and applaud her energy, and she craved for sympathy in all she did.

Their visitors, being accustomed to bright panes as a natural thing, performed by proper functionaries at stated intervals, never thought of admiring Mrs. Cadogan's, who herself thought the windows were well

enough as they were, and it was unnecessary to do more than have them cleaned in
May and November.

The darkness had this advantage certainly, that it partly hid the deficiencies of
the room, for the carpet was threadbare,
and the chair-covers worn and faded; while
the books which lay scattered about the
tables, with no attempt at arrangement, were
not the well-bound, pretty, pictorial works,
such as Travels in the Holy Land, or Views
of Cathedral Towns of England, which are so
suitable for a lady's drawing-room. They
looked as well read as they were ill bound,—
books which other women would have hidden
in some obscure corner, if they had admitted
them into the room at all.

It may be very contemptible, but few
women could be perfectly happy and comfortable with Mrs. Cadogan's shabby, threadbare surroundings. They are affected by

such trivial things in a very absurd way.
That a woman when married should stay
at home, and find all her happiness in her
home-life and the quiet monotony of the
British fireside, is right and proper and
desirable, and the married generally feel
they are in their right place, and come
up to our expectations; but how is it with
the less fortunate daughters of the house,
who have no defined place to fill in the
world? Brought up, it may be, in a luxu-
rious home, where they had at their command all that can please, amuse, and gratify
taste and embellish life, they have been
obliged, when the hey-day was passed, to
leave the home which had been as a Garden
of Eden, and, as maiden ladies, seek some
spot in the wide waste of the world where,
with their high hopes faded, and the vision
of life darkened, they may rest and await
the end. And others, who seek by a mer-

cenary marriage to avoid such a fate, are not less distressing to the beholder.

Beatrice's thoughts, as she sat at the table, were more on the troubles of one woman in particular than with the sex in general.

There had returned to her the sense of the vanity of the world, which had weighed her down at Lucerne; and for the second time in her life she allowed herself to indulge in sentiment.

The pink silk was ruined, and where was she to get another? "Dig I cannot, and to beg I am ashamed," she thought; and, looking life seriously in the face, asked,—

"Was this sort of thing to go on for ever? Was she always to be in need of pink silks?" For, after all, how she is to get these same pink silks, is the great question of a woman's life.

She might marry; and Beatrice dipped her pen into the ink.

She must either marry, or be contented to live without pink silks.

She had arrived at this conclusion, when she was startled by an exclamation from her mother, who, on walking across the room, had caught her foot in a hole in the carpet.

" It must be patched," said Mrs. Cadogan; and it was remarkable how Mrs. Cadogan always used such words on similar occasions, and seemed to suppose that they would have a magical effect. Beatrice sprang from her chair, procured a needle and thread, and began to darn the hole. The employment cheered her, and when her mother drily inquired—" Do you like your occupation?" —her spirits remained undamped.

" I'll mend my pink silk," she said; " and put white over it."

" And won't go to Cadogan, and take the country gentleman's tonic, which, though nasty, is strengthening ? "

"Yes," replied Beatrice, "I shall go to Cadogan; but I'll wait for the Chepstow ball."

"Three hundred a year," thought Beatrice; "a woman should be able to live comfortably on three hundred a year. I am sure I should prefer my crust of bread, my hollow oak and liberty, to any establishment."

"I believe people are much happier when poor," she said, uttering her thoughts aloud.

"So I have heard you say, my dear," was her mother's reply.

Beatrice did write to her uncle that afternoon, and offer to pay him a visit.

She would then determine what she should do, she said; for she would have plenty of time for thought.

CHAPTER VIII.

" Why droops my Lord, like over-ripened corn,
Hanging his head at Ceres' plenteous load ?
Why doth the great Duke Humphry knit his brows,
As frowning at the favours of the world ?
Why are thine eyes fixed to the sullen earth ?
What seest thou there ? "

> *" The oracle within, that which lives,*
> *He must invoke and question."*

MR. CARRICK had drawn his chair to the fire,
and sat smoking his cigar, and meditating on
human life. Apparently, he was inclined to
take a gloomy view of this, for there was a
cloud on his brow, which not even the delicate
fumes of his havannah could dissipate. He
was not an inveterate smoker, but usually he
was susceptible to the soothing influence of

tobacco. The world, indeed, must be very black, and the fates very adverse, when a man refuses to be soothed by his cigar.

Mr. Carrick was aggrieved, and thought he had a just right to be so. He had been hardly dealt with.

He reviewed his past actions, and his conscience told him he had not been desperately wicked; that he had not only kept the Ten Commandments, but had given liberally to the poor. He had been taught to expect that a man reaped as he sowed; but, as far as he could see, his reapings were very different from what they should be. Yet things were going well with him, outwardly. He was doing well in his profession—people even said he was doing wonderfully well. He had a loving mother, pretty sisters, and a comfortable house to come home to every night. He seemed to have little cause for dissatisfaction. Was it that Miss Cadogan had been

K

right, when she said that love was a painful
subject to him?

No. He was not in love. He had experienced that feeling once or twice in his
life before, and he knew that it did not re-
semble that from which he suffered now.
Miss Cadogan's words had not brought a
conscious blush to his cheek, or caused him
the slightest discomposure; so that beyond
a doubt, if he languished in despair, the fairness of a woman was not the cause.

And yet it was.

In point of fact, Mr. Carrick hesitated on
what course of action it was incumbent on
him to take. Two lay open before him,
and their advantages and disadvantages
were so equally balanced, that he could
not say he actually preferred one to the
other.

" Here are two paths," he said, addressing
the chairs and tables; " one of which leads

to Elysium, the other to the other place, and I do not know which is which."

He was not in love, but he thought of marriage.

There was a lady, good-looking, clever, and universally a favourite, and who was a favourite of his own, though he was not in love with her, in one scale; and bachelor-hood—pleasant, agreeable bachelorhood—in the other. The lady was poor; he had paid her some attention, and everybody expected him to make her his wife. But then he thought his attention had been only that of a friend to a very charming woman. Also, he questioned if he did not owe something to himself. A man has to eat for himself, digest for himself, and in general take care of his own dear self, and, therefore, might he not be allowed to live for himself? He did not wish to be selfish, and he wished to do right: but, at the same time, he did not

wish to plunge hurriedly into matri-
mony.

He liked the lady: he thought even that
she would make a most agreeable companion
in this journey through life; but then, if she
married him, it would be for his establishment, for his goods and chattels. And if he
married her, what would he do it for? Not
for her goods and chattels, for she had none;
and not for love, as he had none.

For charity? Yes.

And because it was expected of him? Yes.
But did she expect him to marry her? That
was the question on which everything hung,
and to which he could not give an answer.

Beatrice Cadogan had in no way given
given him to suppose that she expected him
to make an offer of his hand; but still it was
undeniable that she allowed him to approach
her more nearly than any other man. She
talked to him by preference, whenever she

had an opportunity; for even when she had begun a conversation with another person, she would break it to talk with him. It was noticeable, also, that she would even rise from where she was seated, to place herself beside him; and when a young lady acts in this way, it surely must have a meaning?

He admitted that he could not see what there was in this to remark on or blame; he was unable to understand what contamination a young girl could receive from being near him. But still he knew in the world's opinion such an action was to blame, and such contamination considered a point of fact, and therefore he must suppose that she was willing to brave the opinion of the world in order to have the pleasure of sitting near him. When a woman acts in this way, it can surely only mean one thing!

He was not self-conceited; but still he

did not suppose himself to be of so unlovable a nature as to make it unlikely a woman should bestow her regard on him. When Mr. Carrick had come to this conclusion, there seemed but one course open to him— to go to Miss Cadogan, and offer her his hand in marriage.

Having come to this conclusion, Mr. Carrick, in the basest way, pretended he had not.

He now began at the other side of the question, and eagerly brought up the arguments against the step he had proved to be incumbent on him to take as a gentleman and a man of honour. His excuse must be, that he was a lawyer; and I suppose it was a pleasant deception, even though he was the only one deceived, to suppose that he was holding court as a judge, and had on the robes of office.

In the first place, he did not wish to be

married, at the same time desiring that his wishes should go for nothing — absolutely nothing—in the whole affair. He had a most comfortable home, with a mother who thought him perfection, and sisters who allowed him to rule them with a docility which was charming.

If he married, he would not be asked so much into society as he was now, would have to live in smaller rooms, and be contented with a less well-appointed table; for he knew it was a culpable act in a family man of limited means to spend money on the pleasures of good living. And Mr. Carrick was not above being susceptible to these pleasures.

Luxury, he preached, was a very great evil, and when indulged in lavishly became even wicked; but in preaching this he merely did his duty as a British citizen, and was not on that account bound to deny himself his turtle and oysters, his champagne and maraschino, which would decidedly have been carrying virtue too far.

He knew that if he married he would have to relinquish these things, and yet not have the satisfaction of enjoying a sense of his own virtue.

Every man would have agreed with Mr. Carrick that these last arguments far out-weighed the former. Although sacrifice of self is very well in theory, a man is bound first to look after his own person and welfare. If he knew that other men would pay heed to his comfort and regard his wishes, it would be all very well to do the same by them. But, unfortunately, the world is differently constituted. Each individual has, as Mr. Carrick remarked, to eat for himself, digest for himself, and in general take care of his own dear self. Nature has done all in her power to make him selfish, in making his person his castle, in which he immures himself and prepares to sustain the assaults of all who approach. It is curious enough how we still regard all strangers as enemies, and stand on our guard against them until assured that they are very well-meaning individuals.

Hobbes said that man is the enemy of man; and we seem to make his words as true now as ever by our conduct, notwithstanding our advanced civilization and much-talked-of progress. It was Voltaire who said that men's natures are composed of the tiger and the monkey; and at the present day the tiger has whitened his claws, and the monkey laid a thin varnish of philanthropy over his misdeeds. Justice, however, must be done to Mr. Carrick. He wished to act rightly by Miss Cadogan, the world, and himself. His cigar was finished, and his fire had burnt low, and he was not nearer the solution of his difficulty than he had been before.

The judge, having heard the case, had proved himself inefficient, for he was unable to pronounce sentence, and he and the prisoner at the bar might as well have been in bed.

Mr. Carrick determined to think no more of the matter that night. He would act, he said, as the occasion prompted; and so left the final settlement of this, the most important question of his life, to chance. And yet not to chance, for a man's sudden actions are decided by his previous thoughts, deeds, and life. If he has allowed himself to think falsely, his words will involuntarily be false when he is unexpectedly called on to speak. In the same way, our deeds in the past determine our deeds in the future.

CHAPTER IX.

" UNCLE STUART has sent us two wild ducks,"
said Hester, coming into the drawing-room
one evening.

" That is very good of him," said Edward.

" Yes, and we are going to give a party."

" And that will be very good of us. I
suppose, wild ducks being such immense birds,
we must call in our friends to help us to
consume them."

Hester laughed. " It is right we should
give a party," she began.

" I quite agree with you, my dear! It

would be a great pity that others should not enjoy Uncle Stuart's wild ducks as well as ourselves. Do you propose to give us anything else for dinner ?"

" What nonsense, Edward! This is a good opportunity to give a party; and we must do it some time. We can't go and feast with our friends without feasting them too."

" I only made inquiries, my dear, because I thought that, before coming home that day, I should minister to the necessities of nature at an eating-house."

" Don't let us give any parties, dear Hester! Pray don't!" pleaded Louis.

" Oh! Hester, have pity on us! we neither want to feast with other people nor to feast them here," was echoed on all sides.

" I'll consume both wild ducks myself, if you like, dear Hester. Oh! Hester, don't let us give a party," Louis began again.

"Oh! Hester, don't give a party," begged every one.

"I'll tell you whom we shall have," went on Hester, composedly. "We'll not have any elderly people. Edward's wife shall do all that kind of entertainment for us when she comes."

"Yes, when she comes. The elderly people will have to wait some time for their wild ducks, I fear."

"Well, Hester, whom are we to have? You have as yet only told us whom we are not to have," said Ernest.

"Ernest, you see, looks forward to the party with the keenest anticipations of enjoyment," said Hester, her face twisting up in the curious fashion which always betokened amusement.

"On the contrary, Hester, I have been thinking of joining Edward in his refreshment at the eating-house; but I know all our entreaties will pass unheeded,—that when you have once said, ' We must give a party,' there is no hope for us, and the party will be given. Therefore, I ask, which is to be the day, and who the guests?"

" Do have some one of respectable years, Hester, or we shall all forget the dictates of decorum. A grey head would have a sober-ing effect on our spirits," said Cecil.

" Then they shall just not have to be sober."

" Every one must understand," said Anne, " that we cannot give stiff dinner-parties."

" Thank heaven !" was Edward's fervent ejaculation. But his sister continued,—

" Hester is quite right; it will do you all good : you seem afraid of your species."

" Well, Hester, who is to come?" asked Edward again.

" I want to have Miss Cadogan and Mr.

Carrick ;" and her face again twisted up with amusement.

" Hester, Hester, this is shocking ! So young, and yet so full of schemes," cried Louis.

" But I thought," said Edward, " you were going to ask those who feasted us, so that they may feast us again. I don't think either Miss Cadogan or Mr. Carrick has done so."

" Well, Mr. Carrick and Miss Cadogan ; and whom besides ?" inquired Anne.

" Miss Carrick, Miss Evans, and Miss Alison ; Mr. Farebrother, Mr. Willoughby, and Charlie Richards. That will make quite a nice little party."

" And the Miss Aylmers ; you might have them," was Ernest's suggestion.

" Lizzie and Florence ? Let me see, we must get two more men. Harry Macdonald will be in town, and Mr. Murray."

"There, the weighty question is settled," said Cecil.

"And done with, I hope;" and Anne sighed, as though the conversation about it had been very wearisome. "Give me some tea, Hester, and let it be strong," she continued.

"You would be much more comfortable if you would take off your cloak and bonnet, Anne," advised Ernest; for Anne had just returned home as the arrival of the wild ducks was announced.

"Come and sing, Cecil," said Hester, going to the piano. "Anne, you and the boys must join us."

Hester began to play, and Anne hastily swallowed her tea; and, advancing towards the piano with a piece of bread in her hand, joined in the song. Her bonnet was untied, and was pushed on one side of her head; her cloak unfastened, and thrown back on her shoulders: she looked and felt worn out and exhausted; but she forgot this entirely in the pleasure of singing.

The brothers were affected in the same way by the music. They had each a book, and had intended to continue to read, but involuntarily they also began to sing,—

> "Abide with me : fast falls the eventide;
> The darkness thickens ; Lord, with me abide.
> When other helpers fail, and comforts flee,
> Help of the helpless, O abide with me !"

At the last words, " In life, in death, O Lord, abide with me," Anne said, " Now let us have 'Lead, kindly Light'; and, Cecil, get me another cup of tea, and strong."

" Dram drinking ! " said Edward.

" I don't care ; I must have it."

" So says the dram drinker."

" Poor thing, let her have her tea in peace," said Cecil.

" Then give her some food as well."

"No; I only want tea. Well, Hester, go on."

They then sang "Lead, kindly Light."

" Do you know," said Hester, when it was finished, " I found myself rushing about Edward Street to-day, singing psalms; and when I was choosing ribbons, I could only hum, ' Consider the lilies of the field, they toil not neither do they spin,' which seemed strikingly suitable."

Louis, turning again to his book, began,—

" Was macht der Herr Papa."

And the others went on, entering with spirit and animation into the song, and indulging in such gesticulations that any one entering the room would have doubted their sanity,—

" Was macht der Herr Papa,
Was macht der ledere Herr Papa,
Si Sa,
Herr Papa,
Was macht der ledere Herr Papa."

No sooner was this finished than Louis began again, in the most solemn of tones,—

"There were three crows sat on a tree,
And they were black as crows could be,"

—which was again taken up by all present. When the room was quieter again, Ernest said, "I often am surprised Mr. Aylmer does not send in a request that we may enjoy ourselves less noisily."

"He should rather send us his thanks for allowing him to share our fun," said Cecil.

"Well, I trust you may not go on in this way when our friends come to do honour to the wild ducks. If Cecil thinks a grey head would be of any service, I could procure a wig for the occasion."

"No," said Hester; "you shall see how grave and severe I shall be, and, besides, Anne will keep us in order. She is so tired to-night, that she has a mind in common with us, and can only indulge in our silliness."

"I hope my mind is not in common with yours to-night, for your own sakes," said Anne, and sank into a chair.

"More tea, more tea!" cried Cecil.

Hester ran to the table, poured out the cup of tea, while Louis put in cream and sugar, and Edward seized a loaf of bread and a carving-knife.

"I am too tired," said Anne, turning away from the tea.

"Oh, poor dear! This will never do! It must have its tea; now will it, dear?" said Hester.

"And its little piece of bread," cried Edward, brandishing his carving-knife.

Hester got behind her sister, and endeavoured to pour the tea down her throat, while all the others danced round her as though they were Red Indians: Edward and Ernest seemed to have been metamorphosed, and had changed their characters completely.

But I suppose even the gravest of men, when amongst those with whom he has played as a child, forgets at times, and especially under the influence of gaslight, the years which have intervened. Ernest was the first to recollect himself, and, turning away, sat down to his book again, looking as grave and sober, "as though," Hester said, "he had nothing to do with us, and disowned our proceedings."

"Well, write your notes, Hester," said Anne, putting a final end to the affair by leaving the room.

"I have done quite an excellent piece of work," said Edward, with satisfaction. "She will go to her bed much sooner, and we may have some chance of seeing her at breakfast to-morrow."

"A faint chance, I fear," said Cecil. "I am going off, too, or I shan't be down either."

CHAPTER X.

" The guests are met,
The feast is set ;
May'st hear the merry din."—COLERIDGE.

" From all parts they are coming,
As if we kept a fair."—SHAKESPERE.

ON the morning of the day on which the Stuarts were to give their party, Cecil came into the drawing-room, where Hester was busily engaged arranging various matters, and said,—

" My dear Hester, I saw Aunt Charles to-day, and she told me she has not seen you for ten days; and she thinks, considering how near she lives, that it would not take many minutes of your valuable time if you were to look in. Then she sighed,—and you know what it means when Aunt Charles sighs,—'I think, when I have so many nieces, some might come to see me; but no one cares about me. I am neglected and misunderstood on all sides.' "

" It is very odd how Aunt Charles always thinks she is neglected. She would have us, like little dogs, running at her heels all the day," cried Hester, impatiently.

"She is old, we must remember," said Anne, "and make excuses."

" Oh, dear! I hope I shall never be so old that it must serve as an excuse for unreasonableness. Besides, Anne, it is easy for you to make excuses, for she never sends for you."

" Well, Hester, you will never be forgiven if you do not go to her to-day," said Cecil, preparing to set about her own occupations.

" But I can't; it is out of the question. This room must be tidied."

"If you go, I'll tidy the room," said Anne.

"You tidy the room!" was Hester's disdainful reply. "I know what you would do. You would begin with the best possible of intentions : some idea would strike you, and everything else under the sun would vanish from your recollection, until you had worked it out satisfactorily."

"Hester wishes there were no such things as ideas," said Cecil, laughing at her sister's vehemence, who asked immediately after, in tones of despair,—

"Was Aunt Charles quite serious?"

"Quite. She thinks you have used her badly. You are her goddaughter, and owe her certain attention. She is sure she does not ask for much."

"It is most provoking. I suppose her daughters have been fighting! Well, Cecil, I must leave these things to you."

A few minutes later Hester might have been seen hastening down the street, drawing on her gloves and tying her bonnet-strings.

" Where are you going to, so fast?" asked her cousin, Charles Richards, stopping her in her course. He was a small, slight man, with a handsome face, which was spoilt by the colour of his complexion. Like the famous Sir Jacob Kilmansegg,

> " He had roll'd in money, like pigs in mud,
> Till it seem'd to have enter'd into his blood
> By some occult projection ;
> And his cheeks, instead of a healthy hue,
> As yellow as any guinea grew,
> Making the common phrase seem true
> About a rich complexion."

He continued, with a feeble smile,—

" You will give colds to every one whom you pass, you are going at such a pace. You make quite a draught."

" How are you to-day, Charles ? Better, I hope," she said, cheerfully.

" Oh, wretched, wretched ! I have not

slept for nights. I have such lumbago, and the gout in my feet is unbearable."

" I wonder cousin Charlotte let you come out. How is she ?"

"I think she is very well; but she won't hear of it. She says her cough has been more troublesome than usual."

" People who are accustomed to be ill seem to think it quite a luxury, and will never admit that they are better."

" Had they really been ill, had they suffered as I have suffered during these last weeks, it would be very different."

" Well, good-bye: I am going to see Aunt Charles;" and Hester hastened on, thinking that when she left him her cousin seemed to walk more lamely than he had done before. She laughed, too, as she remembered having stayed with him and his sister at their country place, and how it used to be a regular custom that, when the two met in the

morning, they should give a lengthy, sensa-
tional, and minute description of their sufferings during the night.

"Oh, Charles! I had such spasms. I
thought my last moment had come. I rang
for Jamieson, and got some sal volatile, but
it did no good."

"I slept for five minutes between one and
two o'clock, Charlotte; but then was seized
with such violent cramp."

Hester laughed, I say, as she recollected
this; and it is curious how, even to the best
natured, the sufferings of others can cause
amusement.

Mrs. Charles Sidmouth had been a Miss
Stuart, while her husband had been a cousin
of the Aylmers; so that she formed a link
between the two families. She was a handsome woman in appearance; her nephew
Ernest bearing her some resemblance. She
had, however, nothing of his enthusiasm of

character, and the coldness of her steel-grey
eyes struck brave men with terror. She
exaggerated largely both the good and ill
which men did her, and took an equal delight in making out that strangers had
shown her unexampled kindness, and that
friends had injured her grievously. She
was an eager partisan and a bitter enemy.
Her three daughters were of mature years,
and sour in temper. Whenever they were
dull or in want of occupation, it was alleged
that they took to fighting among themselves.
It was, indeed, no unusual thing for one of
them to shut herself up in her room for
twenty-four hours, seeing no one but the
servant who brought her food; the reason
for this being that she had been defeated
in some war of words. They had many
agreeable qualities, and, when apart from
one another, could be entertaining in their
own solemn and grim fashion.

Mrs. Sidmouth never interfered in her daughters' quarrels. "When women come to a certain age they must arrange these matters for themselves," she said; and expected that her nieces should pay her constant visits, in case all her daughters should have felt inclined to shut themselves up at one time. When Hester came into the drawing-room, she found Mrs. Sidmouth sitting in an erect and stately attitude, a book open on a little table before her, and a mark lying ready for insertion.

Mrs. Sidmouth raised her eyes from her page solemnly, and with an expression in them as though it were Sunday, and she was disturbed in her meditations. She put in her mark, closed her book, and rising slowly, and with dignity, advanced to meet her niece, and greeted her with a grave kiss. Hester knew the meaning of this reception, and could have translated it into these words,—

"You have used me badly, and, after all the affection I have lavished on you, I expected better things. Moreover, as your father's sister, I had a right to be differently treated by your father's daughter."

Hester, however, thought her aunt had no reason to feel aggrieved, and that to coax or pet her into good humour would be wrong, and minister to her fancies. She made up her mind, therefore, to be pleasant, cheerful, and amusing.

"Well, Aunt Charles, how have you been?" she asked, and smiled in a bright way, which said, as clearly as words could have done, "I am sure you have been quite well and happy."

"Very well," Mrs. Sidmouth answered, in a manner that implied that she kept back many and important reservations.

"That's right. And the girls?"

"Very well." With the same reservations.

" Have you been reading anything good?"
was Hester's next question.

Mrs. Sidmouth smiled, and replied, in
tones of contemptuous pity,—

" My dear, do you know a modern author
whose writings are good? The trash, the
wretched trash, published now-a-days is inconceivable."

" Oh! do you think so? I only wish I
had time to read all the books published."

Mrs. Sidmouth pursed up her mouth, and
drew in the corners in a way which showed
how most pitiable she considered Hester's
condition to be.

" In my young days," was her reply, "we
read the works of Sir Walter Scott."

" But we read Sir Walter Scott's books,
too," said Hester, her face twisting up
comically.

" There is nothing, nothing in modern
literature which can be compared to his

writings for the beauty of the style, the
healthiness of the thought, and the purity."
Mrs. Sidmouth said these words, leaning forward towards her niece, but in such low,
confidential tones, that Hester could hardly
catch their meaning. Mrs. Sidmouth lived
in constant fear lest the very stones should
prate of her whereabouts. Her movements
were as stealthy as her voice was low and
mysterious. She considered it unladylike,
moreover, to speak above a whisper, and
would frequently reprove Hester for the
vehemence of her tones, saying, "I am not
deaf, my dear," or, "Sweet is a low voice
in woman;" to which last Hester would
reply, "I'd rather be bitter, then, than be
sweet, at such cost to most of my friends."

"I quite agree with you in admiring Sir
Walter Scott's books," she said, and then
looked round, startled by the sound of a
heavy, deep-drawn sigh at her ear. She

saw her cousin, Charlotte Sidmouth, standing in the middle of the room, her arms
hanging limply by her side, and an expression of unutterable misery in the large dark
eyes which were fixed on Hester.

Charlotte Sidmouth was tall, with broad
shoulders and a square figure; about her
head hung short locks, whose auburn colour
was now mixed with white. She was a
clever woman, who wrote and read much, but
spoke little in general society. Indeed, when
at a party, she would frequently look such a
picture of abject misery, that a stranger
might have supposed her to be the victim of
some bitter remorse: she said the cause was
her ill health; but it really was a form of shyness, and the result of eccentricity of temper.

She gave utterance now to a long, deep-
drawn sigh, which could only have proceeded
from the soundest of lungs. "Gracious! what
is that?" cried her mother, and with a sudden,

theatrical start she clutched at Hester's arm.
She heard the same sound a dozen times
a day, but it caused her as much excitement at the recurrence as though it were
perfectly novel and startling.

"Only Charlotte groaning in agony over
the woes of life," said Hester, laughing.
"Come, cheer up, Charlotte, you have not
committed a crime yet." And Hester, spring-
ing from her chair, endeavoured to make
her cousin join in a waltz, but failed to
produce any effect on the immense frame,
which remained immovable as a statue.

"Come and sit down, Hester," commanded
her aunt. "We have really passed the time
of life adapted to frolics. Florence Aylmer
was here to-day," she continued. "She is
a beautiful creature—beautiful." And as
her aunt shook her head, and smiled over
Florence Aylmer's beauty, Hester knew she
was restored to a better humour.

"She is very charming, certainly."

"Oh, beautiful! a beautiful creature—and intellectual. She came and sat with me a long time. She sat there,"—pointing to a seat near,—"and told me all about her thoughts, her reading, and her doings. She was full of Anne's hospital. And Lois came with her,—a bright, vivacious little body, a fine child,—who rattled and talked to me about herself."

Charlotte heaved another sigh.

"What is it this time, Charlotte?" asked Hester. "Things in general, or something in particular?"

"I am sorrowing for Florence Aylmer. She does not believe that the moon stood still at Ajalon."

"She's a good creature," replied Mrs. Sidmouth, "and believes much more than people give her credit for. I have had a long talk with her, and she opened her heart to me."

"I am coming to see Ernest," went on Charlotte. " He believes in his Bible."

"I hope a great many people do," said Hester, gravely.

" Yes, whenever it suits them. They all make mental reservations; but with Ernest I can talk on any subject, however minute, and he follows me with grave concurrence."

" I think you are unjust," began Hester.

" No, I am not. You say you believe everything, and think you do, no doubt; still, were I to talk to you as I do to Ernest, you would laugh, and turn my words into ridicule."

" I hope I should not," said Hester, in distress.

" I daresay you hope, Hester Stuart; but hoping won't do much good. I was speaking to Ernest about the Tables of Stone being handed over to Moses when last we met, and was pleased with his remarks."

"Do you see much of Florence Aylmer, my dear?" asked Mrs. Sidmouth, breaking in again. "I think she would make a good companion for you."

Hester laughed, for she knew that, however she and Florence might like each other, their minds were too little in common for them ever to become companions. She knew also that her aunt thought, that intercourse with Florence might improve her manners, and might even teach her to modulate her voice.

It was shortly after this that Hester returned home.

When all her guests had assembled that evening, she rather regretted the youthfulness of the party after all, and wished there had been some one present over thirty years of age. Ernest took down Miss Evans to dinner. She was a lively, vivacious girl, of about nineteen years of age, a relation of the

Stuarts, though not a native of Sedgeborough. Her only beauty was the quantity of her fair hair, for her face was plain, almost to repulsiveness. She had a sallow complexion, pale green eyes, and a long nose, which seemed to have been unable to determine what shape to take, as it rose and fell at intervals. She spoke in a high voice, rattling out her words as though it were her greatest desire to get rid of them with as much expedition as possible. She had a habit also of shrugging up her slight shoulders to her ears as she spoke. The Stuarts did not like any of the family much,—but then they were relations,—so they never confessed this. It was a point of honour with them to like all their connexions by blood. The Evanses themselves were very different in this matter. Miss Evans declared openly, to any one who would listen, that though she was fond of her brothers she detested her sisters.

"It is so good of you to ask me without Elizabeth," she said to Ernest; "we have been having such fights lately, that we could not have come in the same carriage."

"Poor Mrs. Evans! You should have some compassion for her, Gertrude," was Ernest's reply.

"Oh, poor mamma! she goes dropping her prayers about the house, that we may be converted. She is like the woman in Dickens's ' Tale of Two Cities,' constantly on the flop. I am only surprised her spiritual knees are not worn away by this time."

Ernest was glad after this to turn to Florence Aylmer, who was on his other side. Miss Evans addressed herself to Edward Willoughby, who was her next neighbour, and with whom she had some intimacy, on account of being related. He was very particular about women's appearance, manners, and general conduct, and wished most heartily

he could disown his relationship with Miss
Evans. He was himself very good looking,
and therefore had a right to bq particular,
although, being only one-and-twenty, he had
not yet gained that full command over his long
arms and legs that might have been desirable
for his own ease and self-possession. In
character he was sensitive, impulsive, and
generous, and had an immense amount of
energy of a certain kind, which it was the
desire of his life to exhaust on " something
practical." Combined with this were two
disadvantages: firstly, when he had money
in his pocket, he was never at ease till it
was spent; secondly, when a friend made
him a confidence, he could never rest until
he had imparted it to some other friends in
the strictest confidence.

" I am quite tired of you, Mr. Carrick;
everybody conspires to send us to dinner
together. I am sure we should both agree in

liking a little variety. You can have nothing new to talk about," said Miss Cadogan, as she put her arm into Mr. Carrick's.

" I suppose the reason is, that you always talk to me wherever we may be placed at the table."

" I wonder who my next neighbour will be. Mr. Macdonald, you here! How do you do? I am quite glad to see a face from Cadogan."

Mr. Macdonald, who was the son of one of those county big-wigs whom Miss Cadogan thought so invigorating a tonic, laughingly confessed himself pleased that she should be glad to see him. As he spoke it might have been seen from his manner that he was not without a certain shyness, which probably proceeded from pride and reserve. He was extremely handsome and aristocratic looking, so that Miss Cadogan felt that in talking to him she was in her element; for had he not a lineage which might be compared to her own? Moreover, Miss Cadogan's soul delighted to draw forth his opinions on the subject of "those Radical fellows." She always held that there was nothing more amusing than the conservatism of a true Conservative.

"These sort of things are all very well in theory, but they won't do in practice; that is always what I say, they won't do in practice," he would say, and shake his handsome head sagely, and wave his long white hands in the air to enforce and give effect to his words.

"He has a right to consider himself wise, though," thought Beatrice, laughing at herself; "for has he not inherited his ideas from a long line of ancestors?"

"The shabby way the Government conducts its affairs is shameful," he continued.

"How?" asked Beatrice.

"Oh! in the army, in the navy, and in every department, in fact. I know it has caused great discontent in the army."

"I wish I could hear all about it," said Beatrice; "but I must go with the ladies. You must come and tell me about it afterwards."

In the drawing-room, Miss Evans threw herself on a sofa, saying, "The gentlemen won't be long away, I hope. I feel inclined to go to sleep till they come."

When they came upstairs, Ernest Stuart went immediately to Florence, and, sitting down beside her, remained talking to her for the rest of the evening. They had found some subjects on which they could agree, and Ernest was gradually led on to speak of his own life and work as he had never spoken of them to any other person. He had met Florence several times since they had been to the hospital together, and every meeting had served to increase the interest in her which had then been aroused. Unconsciously he began to alter the force and meaning of her words to him on former occasions; so that he saw now in her talk about light and culture a sign of the purity and beauty of her nature. "It is possible for women like her," he said to himself, "to tread on this ground, because their own character will save them from the evil consequences which would come to others. I see how I misunderstood her." Florence intentionally avoided those subjects on which she knew they could not agree, and was quite unaware that she had led him to make a mistake as to her real opinions.

"Miss Cadogan," said Mr. Carrick, "are you not going to say a word to me?"

"No, I am tired of you. Lizzie Aylmer is going to sing; go and turn over her leaves. Mr. Willoughby, how mournful you look; is anything wrong?"

"How?" asked Edward, and allowed his long eyelashes to fall over his cheek in a way which plainly said he thought it was a liberty on Miss Cadogan's part, which he felt bound to resent, to make any remark on his personal appearance.

" I ask why? and you ask 'how?' in return. Your questions are most enigmatical. By the bye, Mr. Stuart," she continued, addressing Louis, "I have to call on the Miss Sidmouths; but I should like to know first what condition of spirits I am likely to find them in. Can you tell me?"

" Low, low," said Louis, shaking his head.

" They are the most entertaining people I know."

" I am glad you should be entertained by my cousins."

" Now, Mr. Stuart, that is too bad. Everybody is a cousin of yours, I believe. You cannot expect us always to remember that. Mr. Macdonald, are you a cousin of Mr. Stuart? I suppose so."

"No," he replied, laughing, and shaking his head.

"Indeed! wonderful! Then, Mr. Stuart, we may talk of Mr. Macdonald."

"Suppose we don't talk of any one?"

"Oh, yes, but I want to speak of Mr. Macdonald. What has he been doing with himself lately, do you know?"

"Enjoying himself, I suppose."

"Yes, thank you, Miss Cadogan, I have been enjoying myself very well."

"Of course you have. You are an eldest son, and the whole arrangement of society is constituted to minister to the enjoyment of an eldest son."

"Won't you speak to me now, Miss Cadogan?" asked the indefatigable Mr. Carrick, returning to the charge.

"There are Lizzie and Florence Aylmer going; so I am going to take my departure under their wings."

"Your carriage has been announced."

Beatrice said good-bye to the Stuarts, and went from the room with the Aylmers and Ernest Stuart.

"Is your carriage here, Miss Cadogan?" he asked.

"Yes, here in point of fact—my carriage and pair. I walk home with my maid." She then bade them good-night, and walked towards her home with her servant.

It was not long, however, before Ernest joined her.

"You must let me come with you," he said.

"Did you see the Aylmers safely home?" she asked, looking at him critically. The light of the street lamp fell on his face, and she could have sworn he blushed.

"Florence was most beautiful to-night," she said again.

"Yes," he answered slowly; "she is beautiful."

"I hope she will never marry; it would spoil her," she said next.

"How wet the roads are," he exclaimed, in hopes of changing the conversation.

"You'll wet your feet: you had better go back."

He laughed.

"No, I thank you."

"Don't you agree with me that it would spoil her if she were ever to marry?"

"I have really not thought on the subject."

"She wore blue to-night. Do you not like the colour?"

"Yes, I like the colour," he replied; all astray as to what she might mean.

She laughed. "This is our house. Good-night, and thanks for your company. I hope neither of us will dream of blue angels." And Beatrice went into the house.

"How they enjoyed themselves as they sat apart," she thought; "but they were both unconscious of it till I put it into his head. They are ignorant of these things, poor dears!"

Beatrice's warning about the blue angels had been in vain. Ernest was like nothing so much as a high-mettled horse, which, having the bit between his teeth, will dash forward in a mad career. He had seized his idea, and nothing could stop him in his course or give him pause. His idea was that Florence Aylmer was the purest and fairest creature the world had ever seen; that their former differences of opinion had arisen from his being unable to comprehend her finer nature.

"What a life such a woman might lead!" he thought, and this was only a step from the thought, "What a life a man might lead with such a woman for his helpmate!" With men like Ernest such steps are quickly taken; they rush on from one idea to another, until they have created a fabric of so unsubstantial and illusive a nature, that it is unable to endure the weight of their faith, and falls beneath it. The question is, will the faith be crushed with the illusion, or rise trium phant, either to form another or to gain wisdom and stability?

In the struggle which ensues in their nature there is always something tragical, for is it not a question of life or death—the life or death of the soul?

To Ernest the world had suddenly become beautiful—a dream, a poem. When he awoke to the sternness of the reality, would he have strength to survive the shock?

CHAPTER XI.

"Come down, O maid, from yonder mountain height:
What pleasure lives in height (the shepherd sang),
In height and cold, the splendour of the hills?
But cease to move so near the heavens, and cease
To glide a sunbeam by the blasted pine,
To sit a star upon the sparkling spire;
And come, for love is of the valley; come,
For love is of the valley; come thou down
And find him."—PRINCESS.

WHEN people live next door in a town like Sedgeborough, it is wonderful how frequently they are thrown together, or how often they are reminded in one way or the other of each other's existence.

The true foundation, it must be remembered, of an ideal like that which Ernest was forming of Florence Aylmer is thought; so

that it was much more important to its
growth that he should be made to think of
her, than that they should meet often or talk
much. The intercourse which they had held
together had been sufficient to arouse a
mutual interest; and there being between
them, notwithstanding the differences in
their characters, some natural affinity, this
interest unconsciously grew and ripened in
each.

Florence was aware that without a certain
exclusiveness a man cannot work; that as
soon as he begins to see side-truths and side-
lights his strength in action is weakened.
Ernest, she saw also, had many, and even
brilliant abilities. He was a first-rate classical scholar, and his studies in this direction
were to him of absorbing interest. He would
have been well content could he have chosen
an occupation which would have had some
connexion with these; and even now, if he

took up one of the works of a favourite author, it would warm him to such enthusiasm that he found it difficult to lay it down at the call of duty. He had a keen and delicate sense of any artistic literary beauty; and in this he and Florence had much in common. He could speak to her of the books or particular passages he admired, and could be certain that he would not be met with the high-bred, quiet ridicule with which any expression of real feeling is treated in society.

To Florence also, it must be remembered, it was rare to come in contact with a man who thought there were more important and interesting topics of conversation than what Mr. or Mrs. So-and-So did, and what Miss So-and-So said. He never thought of discussing his neighbours, or of restricting conversation in the approved fashion to passing and outward events. She could feel sure he really meant what he said, and did not

talk the jargon of a particular set; the forms
and phrases of society having no importance
in his eyes.

I suppose she cannot have been wholly
uninfluenced by his good looks and the
charm of his manner; for not even those to
whom his intolerance was obnoxious could
deny that he had a certain fascination. He
had an old-world chivalry of nature and
courtesy of demeanour towards all whom he
might meet, and we must admit that

> " Manners are not idle, but the fruit
> Of loyal natures and of noble minds."

It must be recollected also that, though a
curate, he had nothing in common with the
ordinary type of his class which is familiar
to us all: a man who has taken orders for
an employment, and who is associated in our
minds with croquet, gossip, and clerical jokes,
and whose greatest ambition is to be popular
in the society into which he is thrown.

One afternoon, Lois went into Lizzie's room, and, after fumbling about the table, as though in search of something lost, said, confidentially, " Do you know, Lizzie, I think Florence is in love ! "

Lizzie looked up, laughing.

" With a new work on calorific rays ? " she asked.

" No, that 's just it; don't you see ? "

" No, I am sorry I don't."

" Why, Lizzie, you are stupid! " cried Lois, impatiently. " Don't you see, she has had some learned volume on her knee the whole morning, and yet has been constantly staring out of the window in a brown study."

" And that is a sign of love, is it ? "

" Yes, of course; don't you know? " was the eager answer. " You feel happy, and then you get doleful, then happy again. am sure Florence is in love. I have seen her smile constantly, which usually she never does when reading. I am sure I don't wonder, considering what she reads; and then she gets quite grave, and sighs a little, and turns over a page, of which, I am sure, she does not know one syllable."

"How do you come to know the meaning of these wonderful signs? One would imagine your own experience had been lively."

"You are too silly, Lizzie! I have seen them often in others; and, besides, I know them perfectly."

"Well, remember not to tell everybody what your fancies are."

"They are not fancies."

Miss Frost was also dissatisfied with Florence at this time; but she did not seem so conversant with the signs of love as Lois, for she puzzled over these same fits of abstraction, but could find no cause to account for them. Florence looked well in health, and Miss Frost was utterly incapable of understanding how any one not dangerously ill could fail to be absorbed in a new scientific work. She thought, for her own part, that, even were she dying, a brochure would recall her to life.

"Mrs. Aylmer, have you noticed anything wrong about Florence?" she asked, one day. "She is not like herself at all. Last Sunday afternoon, when she came to read to me, she was quite abstracted. I could see her mind was elsewhere."

"I dare say," said Mrs. Alymer, in reply, "that she has had enough of reading for a time. It is generally noticeable with girls of her age, that a reaction sets in, and they abjure for a space what they have liked before."

"But there must be some reason," persisted Miss Frost. "Such a reaction in Florence would be quite unaccountable."

"The reason is to be found in satiety, I think."

" I could understand that, were it satiety of parties, balls, or amusements generally."

" But not of thought ? Can't you really? Reading and thought have been to Florence what amusements are to other girls, and she has got tired of them, I suppose, as they tre of these."

" I cannot say I am satisfied. Have you really not seen that there is something wrong, Mrs. Aylmer ? I am sure Lois has. She talks constantly of 'the fair and abstracted Florence.' "

" Here comes Lizzie, we'll ask her. Lizzie, is there anything wrong about Florence ?"

" Lois says she is in love, mamma," said Lizzie, laughing.

" The stupid, silly child !" cried Miss Frost, indignantly. " How she gets such notions about love, I don't know; but it is too much when she would give them to Florence also."

" Yes, she certainly could not have fixed on any one more unlikely than Florence to be affected in that way. I am sure, Miss Frost, it is only relaxation the child requires."

" But she has not worked much for a month, at least."

" It may be, then, she requires work," said Mrs. Aylmer, laughing. " But I believe, for my part, there is nothing wrong with her at all."

Miss Frost had no doubt that, whatever the nature of Florence's complaint might be, work would be good for her. She therefore determined to reason with her, and point out that she had been going astray, and took the first opportunity of following her to her room, and speaking on the subject.

" Florence," she said, " I have been very anxious about you, and quite unable to understand your conduct. You have been wasting your time."

Florence laid her hand affectionately on Miss Frost's shoulder, as she answered,—

"I have not been wasting my time. I have been learning, only I have had another teacher."

"Another teacher?" repeated Miss Frost, in tones of quick resentment and jealousy.

"Yes; and have been learning most necessary lessons."

"And your teacher?"

"Has been life," she replied. "It has taught me that there are more important things for me than scientific or philosophical studies."

"More important? Florence! what do mean?"

"That a life would be ill spent which had only individual learning for its end; but cases are very different, Miss Frost. You influence and train the minds of others, while I remain absorbed in my thoughts, which can have no use, and which have, indeed, given me so far an isolated existence. The lesson I have learnt is that we must all work; the lesson I have still to learn is what my work is to be."

"This mania about woman's work and sphere and usefulness,—has it touched you too, Florence?" cried Miss Frost, in exasperation.

"Yes; and it seems to me that every woman must be touched by it. You have found out your sphere of usefulness, and I must find mine."

"Then what do you propose to do?"

"You are vexed with me, I see, and disappointed; but you must make excuses for a time. I have known and understood so little the significance of life, that what knowledge I have gained has come as a revelation to me."

"You have come to no determination, then?"

"To none except this. I have resolved to enter more into the interests of other people; but, at the same time, I do not in the least intend to give up reading."

After this conversation, Florence made an effort to rouse her mind from abstraction to active thought. It is no exaggeration to call this an effort on her part; for when a mind is occupied with personal affairs, it is almost impossible that it should turn with ready interest to an obscure or difficult study. Florence succeeded so well, however, as to satisfy Miss Frost, and assure her that a "little rousing" had been all that was necessary.

CHAPTER XII.

"O beautiful creature, what am I
 That I dare to look her way?"—TENNYSON.

"The drift of the matter is dark, an Isis
 Hid by a veil."—TENNYSON.

"At war with myself and a wretched race;
 Sick, sick to the heart, of life am I."—TENNYSON.

ONCE, when Florence went to see Mrs. Sidmouth, she had been asked by her to visit a poor woman who was dying of consumption. and take her a few delicacies.

"I heard of her some time ago as being in great necessity, and gave her work to do, which was an assistance. She was so grateful, poor thing! But her health has failed completely since then. She has come through many trials, and it may do her good to see a young and kind face," Mrs. Sidmouth had said.

So Florence, one afternoon, accompanied by her maid, who carried wine and jelly, went to Brompton Lane, where Mrs. Blake lived.

She was directed to go two stairs up; and taking the basket from the servant's hand, and bidding her wait outside, she went in.

It was a low and wretched room, into which the small, dark window scarcely allowed any light to penetrate; two panes were broken, but the apertures were so closely stuffed with rags, that not a breath of air could enter to purify the fœtid atmosphere. This room Mrs. Blake shared with six others. When Florence came in, however, there were only two occupants.

Mrs. Blake was lying on a miserable chaff bed, which looked as though it had seen many generations. She was pale and ema-

ciated, gasping for every breath convulsively;
and Florence, as her eyes rested on her, felt,
with a sense of dread, that death must be
near. She saw also, bending over the
woman, the slight, well-known figure of
Ernest Stuart. He was speaking in low,
eager tones, and she hesitated whether to
advance or not; but he, too, had seen her, and
came towards her, with a flush rising to his
cheek—for was she not now fulfilling his ideal?

The moment after, his thoughts, however,
returned to the suffering woman, whose
chances of eternal life or death were hanging
in the balance.

" Flor —Miss Aylmer," he said, in tones of
suppressed eagerness, " go to her, and speak
to her; it is her last chance of salvation.
You may have more, you must have more,
power than I."

He took the basket from her hand. " She
cannot eat anything," he said; "I have tried."

Florence then stepped forward to the bedside, while Ernest went to the window so that she might feel unembarrassed in her talk. He turned to look at her for one moment, as she leant over the bed. It was almost the last time that he saw his ideal in Florence Aylmer; and, as he looked at her, he told himself she was hardly human in her purity and perfection.

Florence told the woman how Mrs. Sidmouth, on hearing of her illness, had sent her.

"Aye," she said, "I'm near my end."

"And near the haven of rest."

"They tell me no."

"Then they tell you wrong; death must bring rest and comfort."

"I canna say I believe I am forgi'en."

"But your sins are forgiven you."

"The torment o' hell," murmured the woman, between her parched lips.

"There is no such place; it is only in our own minds: we suffer from it here. We shall all be brought to heaven hereafter."

The words were hardly uttered before the woman drew a long, gasping breath, clutched at her arm, and then sank back rigid.

"Mr. Stuart!" cried Florence; and Ernest came forward, and saw that all was over. The room had become very dark to Florence; she felt faint and giddy, so that it was only with a great effort that she retained her self-command.

Ernest led her to the door. "If you go, Miss Aylmer," he said, "I shall join you immediately. I must first speak to the neighbour who was with her when I came."

Florence found her way downstairs, slowly and with difficulty; but Ernest joined her before she got into the street.

They walked on silently for some time, Florence feeling that utterance of any kind was impossible, for it was the first time she had been in presence of death,—and what a death!

She felt, too, that Ernest had been to blame for having embittered the last moments of a life, the end of which would have been sad enough at any rate.

Ernest spoke first.

"Dreadful," he said, "to think how often in this life we are too late! It might have been a soul saved." Then she turned to him, a faint colour tinging her pale cheek, and her voice thrilling with indignation,—

"You think that woman was created to live miserably here and suffer torment hereafter; and you can worship the Being you consider capable of such a creation? Do you not know, Mr. Stuart, that your creed of Christianity, if it has a meaning, means this—that a perfect man was born who conquered death? Eternal death is not an existence to which men are doomed in their life hereafter; it is estrangement from the Divine Being, from which we must suffer more now than in the future."

"If Christianity means anything? And my creed? Florence,—Miss Aylmer,—what do you mean?"

"You have been worshipping a Being of your own creation, who would simply have been human had not inordinate power made him inhuman."

"Miss Aylmer," and his face became white to his lips, whilst his long, slender hands were tightly clenched, "do you know what you say?" His ideal, which had become part of his very nature, lay shattered at his feet.

"Yes," she answered firmly, "I know what I say, and feel it more strongly than I have expressed it."

"Miss Aylmer, you do not believe," he began, and then stopped, continuing again after a pause, his words being forced out painfully,—" you do not believe in the Atonement, and that through faith alone we are saved ?"   .

" I certainly do not think that belief in a doctrine can save us."

" It is the one essential thing."

" Then you believe," she said, " that all who do not hold the Christian faith shall not enter the kingdom of heaven?   I should prefer to be in your hell to your heaven; it would be the better place."

" Miss Aylmer, I entreat of you to recollect what you say.   You deliberately reject the revelation which the Divine Being has given us of Himself—deliberately, and with open eyes."

" If I have rejected any truth," was her answer, " it is not a wilful rejection.   What I wish you to recognize is this : that God has many ways besides the narrow one which we take to draw men to Himself. We must not limit His power by our systems and creeds."

"Great God!" he cried, the words wrung from him in the strength of his passion. "Do you not see you have turned aside from the simple truth, 'Strait is the gate, and narrow is the way, which leadeth unto life?' It is terrible to see you philosophizing calmly on the brink of destruction."

"How is it possible you can retain a creed like this, mixing in life as you have done? It is far more terrible, believe me, than my calm philosophy, that you should be able to preserve your reason; you who have seen numbers of your fellow men who have lived in sin and ignorance die without any sense of the divine existence, holding that death is eternal."

"We cannot answer as to the fate of those who have not been shown the truth here."

"You speak of the truth," she said, in calm

surprise, "as though it could be grasped by a human mind!"

He went on paying her no heed.

"But as for those who have rejected the truth openly and deliberately for the wisdom of the world, we have been told, in clear, unmistakable words, the future that awaits them. Miss Aylmer, I conjure you, I beg of you, to think of this. Were you to die now"—he was unable to continue. He could not pronounce sentence openly on the woman whom he loved, and yet he knew he must pronounce sentence on her to himself. Were she to die, she could not be saved; she was at enmity with God. For the woman who had died so short a time before in the darkened room, in miserable circumstances, there might be some hope of mercy; for he could not tell whether she had ever had a chance or not of receiving the truth, as he called it. But for Florence Aylmer there was no such hope. She had rejected the Divine guidance, and had chosen her own path; had preferred the wisdom of men to that of God. And this was the woman whom he had loved—his ideal of all that was true and noble!

Had he been a weaker man, he would have shrunk from drawing the conclusions of his creed home to what concerned himself. He would have made excuses for Florence, and invented many ways by which she could escape from the judgment he would have pronounced on others. But Ernest Stuart, knowing that were she a stranger he would condemn her, condemned her, though she had won his love.

Experience had brought home to him the full bitterness of his creed, and even-handed justice commended the ingredients of the poisoned cup to his own lips which he had before commended to others. He was strong, and did not turn aside as another might have done, but drank the poison to the dregs, his very strength lending bitterness to the draught.

Was it not true what she had said, that in his hell would be found more righteous men than in his heaven? Now he saw the full blackness of the world his imagination had created. He saw an angry and revengeful God, seated on the throne of power, who had permitted the blood of the innocent to be shed for a few elect, and who had created millions for destruction. He saw Florence Aylmer as he had seen her bending over the bed of the dying woman, and he recalled the fair and noble beauty of her face, and knew that they were separated for ever by an unfathomable gulf; for he was not made of so slight a stuff as to be able to throw the creed of his youth and his manhood aside at the first shock his faith encountered. The rains descended, the floods came, the winds

blew, and beat on his house, and it did not
fall. The question was, would it fall even-
tually? and falling, what would be left? Had
he strength sufficient to arise to new life out
of the destruction of the old? Had he enough
elasticity and adaptiveness of character to
build a new edifice ?

He hardly knew how they reached home,
or how they separated. As he paced about
his room, struggling for composure and submission, it was a relief to remember that in
two days' time he must return to London.
He would thus be able to forget his own
troubles in working to save others as lost as
Florence Aylmer. The thought then came
to him that he must make one effort to save
her. Common humanity would give him the
right to do so, putting the claims of his love
aside. He seized a pen, and wrote as follows :

" After what has passed between us, I
cannot leave this without making an effort

to influence you. I beg of you, Miss Aylmer, as a man who has given you his love and trembles for your eternal welfare, to consider well your position, and the reasons for which you have rejected the Divine Revelation. If you do this truthfully and earnestly, it cannot be in vain.

"ERNEST STUART."

It was nothing to him that he had no right to address her; he knew her well enough to be aware that she was incapable of feeling any offence at his conduct.

END OF BOOK FIRST.

BOOK SECOND.

"O'er strange lands, across the sea,
My falcon has come back to me."

E. D. CROSS.

CHAPTER I.

" A spirit fit to start an empire,
And look the world to awe."

IT was about the time that these occurrences were taking place in Sedgeborough, that Maurice Aylmer had occasion to visit Oxford. He went to see a ward of his, who was an undergraduate at Balliol, and arrange some business matters with him.

After he had transacted this, it recurred to his mind that Sydney Aylmer was at Christ Church, and that he might do well to employ what time he had yet at his disposal in going to see him.

On making inquiries, he found that his cousin was at home, and was shown up to his room.

It was many years since they had met, and Maurice remembered having been rather repelled by the brusquerie of the red-haired, undeveloped youth, whose individuality seemed to run counter to that of most other people. He knew, however, that men who are polished in their manners and adaptive in their character at eighteen years of age have seldom stuff enough in them to form afterwards anything but the most commonplace of beings, and probably experience of life and association with other men had softened Sydney's eccentricities. Moreover, Sydney's father was the nearest relation Maurice Aylmer had, and was the heir-presumptive to his property. "No doubt," he thought, "Sydney will have inherited a certain amount of eccentricity;"

and smiled a little as he recalled to mind a long walk in the rain he had enjoyed with Mr. Aylmer some years ago, when he had been quite a lad. They had shared the same umbrella; and Mr. Aylmer broad, and Maurice slight, in these days, the wet drops had dripped down his neck or on to his shoulder. Moreover, his attempts to cheer the way by conversation were met by chilling monosyllabic replies; so that from these attempts he soon desisted, wishing, with all the impetuosity of these times, his cousin would be civil, if he chose to use his umbrella.

Maurice Aylmer had been very different then from what he was now, at the age of thirty-five. A picture of him, painted at that time, is hanging in the dining-room at Aylmer Court. It represents an eager, impetuous boy, who looked out into the world as though he would not rest until he had found the secret of existence, or would beat out his strength in a passionate endeavour to do so. The thinness of the face gave undue prominence to the square broad forehead, aquiline nose, and piercing grey-blue eyes. It was a striking face, but would never have led any one to suppose that he would be the handsome man he afterwards became.

He was six feet three in height, but the proportions and symmetry of his form were perfect. The square head was splendidly set on the broad shoulders. Strangers were always struck by a fashion he had of facing round completely if he wished to see anything or address any one. His movements all appeared to be slow, measured, and well considered; but he had an advantage over others in this, that from his immense size and strength of limb he required half the time and half the exertion for his actions which other men used. His features were well cut, but massive,—the fairness of his complexion presenting a striking contrast to the straight black hair, which he wore divided in the centre, and the dark eyes. The lower part of his face was completely concealed by the long curling beard which swept across his breast. Of this beard he was particularly proud. There was not another in Europe, he said, which could be compared to it.

His whole appearance gave you the impression of immense power and repressed strength, moral and physical,—of a man who would not be lightly turned away from any object he had in view, and yet who, if convinced it were wise to desist, would desist. He had found the secret and motive of his own being, and by this had gained

> "Self-reverence, self-knowledge, self-control."

He had learnt to act

> "The law he lived by without fear,
> And because right is right, to follow right."

The impetuosity and passion in the boy had been trained by the man into perseverance and earnestness. Of course, entire self-subjection can never be gained, and even yet he could be led away by the moment's impulse, and a fire, not entirely under his control, would kindle within him.

Maurice Aylmer had been left alone in the world, with an immense fortune at his disposal, when he was only seventeen years of age. His guardian and cousin, Mr. Aylmer, was disposed to leave his management as much as possible in his own hands.

" He did not wish to be burdened with strange young men," he said; "he had a wife to look after, which was as much as could be expected of any man. And as for the property, he had never had any of his own to manage, and did not see why he should have all the trouble now of learning the trade, and none of the advantage."

Aylmer Court was a large property, in the Lake country, which had been in the hands of the present family for many generations; but, besides this, Maurice succeeded to £30,000 a year.

Maurice's father had only had one sister, a widow in these days, a Mrs. Radnor, and his wife had died very shortly after their only son's birth.

When Mrs. Radnor heard of her brother's death, she hastened to Aylmer Court to see her nephew, and advise his guardian as to his future career, which, considering his wealth and position, was not one to be entered on lightly.

Mrs. Radnor was a thoroughly kind-hearted woman, but I doubt whether she would have hastened to console her nephew with the same eagerness, or felt so deep a sympathy in his loss, had it not been for this same £30,000 a year. She would have been very

sorry for the "poor boy," but would have
uttered many more platitudes about loss
being common to the race, and its having
a strengthening effect on a young man's
character if he set forth in life fully aware
of its hardships. Mrs. Radnor would have
denied this strenuously, and with much
genuine indignation; but she had practised
petty falsenesses so long in society, that it
was not surprising that she should be also
false to herself. She was a handsome woman,
on whom her fifty-two years had not left
many traces of care. She was full of energy
and restlessness and ambition of a small
kind. She was ready at any moment to
start on a journey of any length, for any
reason whatever; indeed, so far did she
carry this, that it almost developed into a
mania. It was alleged against her that she
had once gone to Paris to get a piece of
black ribbon; and her nephew would never

have been surprised had he met her unexpectedly in any of the four quarters of the
globe in which he might chance to be travelling. There was noticeable in her high-
toned voice a certain peevishness and bitterness, which told of many disappointed hopes
and desires. Her life had not been pillowed
so softly, after all, as it seemed to be, and
weariness and disappointment may have
caused this restlessness of spirit, which was
always seeking exhaustion in what was too
often useless and thankless labour. The good
nature which I have mentioned was quite
the chief characteristic of her disposition;
and if she thought a person more worthy to
be served who had a title and rank, it was as
much a fault of her intellect as of anything
else. She really had a most sincere compassion for any one who did not know a
countess. She thought seriously that such
people belonged to a lower creation, and it

was natural enough that she should have most sympathy with those whom she considered were of her own species.

Maurice Aylmer, at seventeen years of age, was handsome, rich, and alone in the world, and therefore Mrs. Radnor hastened to lavish her affection and care on him.

Mr. Aylmer, gloomy and miserable at being torn away from his natural sphere to look after a stray youth whom he had never seen before, and whom he never cared to see again, was willing enough that Mrs. Radnor should dictate to him what was to be done. As far as he could see, she and Maurice were the most suitable people to decide on the matter, and he would be thankful if they would take it from his hands altogether.

"Maurice must go into the Guards," said Mrs. Radnor. "He might get into his cousin Lord Lake's regiment."

"But when there is no chance of fighting,

aunt, I do not see the advantage of the army as a profession."

Mr. Aylmer smiled grimly at the boy's innocence.

" My dear boy," and Mrs. Radnor smiled too, " young men in your position join the Guards in order to see life and get into society. Not that there would be any difficulty in your getting into society under any circumstances."

" By society, being always understood," put in Mr. Aylmer, " a certain set in London where people are called Lord and Lady instead of Mr. and Mrs."

Maurice wished to see life, and naturally supposed that in society it could best be seen. He therefore declared his ambition was to become a Guardsman; and the affair was settled. Mr. Aylmer completed all the arrangements of the place under Mrs. Radnor's directions, and proved himself so

malleable to her will, that she became convinced the poor man was really sensible,
though he had no chance of entering society.

" You· must leave the house as it is at
present, Maurice," she said, looking round
the large handsome drawing-room, with its
heavy old-fashioned furniture; " for of course
you won't be here much.   We must leave all
refurnishing to your wife. . I hope you will
marry well, Maurice; all your people have
married well."

So Maurice went into the Guards, and lived
the life that is natural to young and wealthy
barbarians. As his aunt would say, he entered
society and saw life,—which means that he
was shown many evil ways, and spent his
days in hunting, shooting, betting, &c.   But
even during these years he did not abandon
himself entirely to the animal enjoyment of
life; but seeing the shallowness and exclusiveness of the set which was all the world to

his aunt, he kept up his interest in other concerns. He had seen active service in the Crimea, and what he saw there of life excited in him a desire to see more of men and the world than society could ever show him.

When he was seven-and-twenty, he left the army, and the last ten years of his life were spent in travelling and in gaining wisdom; for he did not travel as a sportsman in search of adventures to relieve the monotony of existence, but as a man anxious to see all the different phases of life, and learn from them what he could. Nor was he, on the other hand, that aimless being, a man without ambition, travelling vaguely in search of knowledge. He was thoroughly practical, and would have agreed entirely with Hester Stuart's authority, Helmholtz, in saying, that " Das Wissen allein ist aber nicht Zweck des Menschen auf der Erde," and " Nur das Handeln giebt dem Manne ein würdiges

Dasein"; and in the world of literature he
was well known as the author of many useful
and able works. The well-being of humanity
was not so much a passion with him as it was
with Ernest Stuart. It was rather the object
of his well-regulated desires. But then it
must be remembered that he was a tolerant,
large-minded man, who did not suppose that
the greater part of his species were hurrying
to destruction. He saw clearly the failure of
man even in his best endeavours; and knew
that—

> " The best
> Somehow eludes us, ever still might be,
> And is not."

But this did not blind him to the positive
good that may be found. His influence over
others was greater than that of Ernest, because
of his wider sympathies, based on a character
which was really stronger. The one man
was idealistic, sensitive, and morbid; the
other, rational, grave, and self-contained.

Maurice might have been thought "high, self-contained, and passionless"; but it was not so, for he had beneath the calm exterior a nature full of fire and passion, which he had curbed to his will.

Major Aylmer found his cousin Sydney changed beyond all recognition, and he could hardly have believed that the fair-haired man before him was the brusque, ill-mannered boy of so few years back. Although the exclusiveness of the Oxford world, with its want of broad human interest, had not been as favourable a school for Sydney as might have been chosen, it had developed him wonderfully; or, perhaps, the developing power had been laten in his character. He was still intolerant in a sense of other worlds and interests than his own, though his intolerance was toned down, especially in expression. He hated what was called society, and a party was weariness and vexation of spirit to him.

With regard to amusements of this nature, he might have said, with Sir George Cornewall Lewis, that life would be very tolerable if it were not for its pleasures. But, on the other hand, he had a lively appreciation of many pleasures of life. The study of natural science in all its branches was a keen delight; wherever he went he carried his microscope with him, so that his sister Lois called it his shadow. He enjoyed also a lively sense of his own wisdom and good sense, which latter quality he believed to be about the highest a man could have. He despised idealism, and was pleased when he could take one of his sisters to task for rhodomontading, as he called it; and at the expression of any feeling on their part, he would ejaculate " Stuff," with much vehemence.

For the rest, he was methodical, precise, clear-sighted, and persevering, with more of the tortoise than the hare in his disposition.

He was of a small, slight person, which was always carefully and nattily dressed. His manner of walking gave him something of the appearance of a diminutive steam-engine; his steps were short, quick, and very characteristic. His hair had lost much of its redness of shade, even in his whiskers and moustache, which, it is true, did not yet present any very formidable appearance. His eyes were full of expression; in colour they were of that peculiar steel-blue which is generally seen only accompanying a critical, sarcastic disposition. He was short-sighted, and always went about with spectacles fixed on a nose, the shape of which was not even to his own satisfaction. The two cousins had a long talk on many subjects; at the end of which Sydney said,—

" You never come our way, do you?"

" To Sedgeborough? No; I have not been there for many years."

"Well, Aylmer Court is not very far off; and if you are ever down there, we should be happy to see you. I shall be down there at Easter, if you care to come."

A quick flush came over Major Aylmer's face, as all the vague possibilities of such a visit occurred to him.

"Thank you," he replied; "I shall be at the Court then, and shall be happy to go to Sedgeborough. I should know some of my relations."

"My people will be glad to see you, I am sure," said Sydney.

Maurice, as he went away, felt glad that he should have an opportunity of seeing Miss Cadogan again. "What if she be married?" he thought; and the question came with quick pain.

He might disapprove of Beatrice in many ways, and see that she was a woman who would not make his life happy in the comfortable, easy sense of the word. But, then, life was not meant to be spent in sitting still, eating and drinking; and it might be a question if a union with Beatrice would not conduce to their mutual advantage. He recognized that there was a certain affinity between them; and was this a thing to be put aside?

The case would have been different had she merely exercised a fascination over him,— he would have been able to free himself from the influence of this at once,—or had it been from their having been thrown together that their intimacy had arisen. He had been brought into as close connexion with other women, and they had not influenced him as Beatrice had done. The simple feeling which prompts a man to throw down a book or a newspaper to talk to a woman, and the *laissez aller* which leads this talk to other talk about eternal ties and knots which are not to be cut here or hereafter, would not have ruled him. He really believed that a woman whom a man chooses to be his wife should be chosen for some other reason than that she has made an agreeable companion during a short journey, and has talked to him pleasantly about the weather and things in general.

This may have arisen from his belief that a wife enters into a man's interest, that he takes her really for better for worse, and not to become simply a domestic machine and household manager.

It might be well, therefore, that Beatrice Cadogan should become his wife without respect to her wisdom and goodness.

CHAPTER II.

"Changelings and fools of Heaven, and thence shut out,
Wildly we roam in discontent about."—DRYDEN.

BEATRICE CADOGAN was glad when it was finally fixed that she should spend some time with her uncle. Her depression and despondency increased in an unaccountable manner with every day that she remained at Sedgeborough, so that her mother said,—

"I am sure I shall be thankful to get you away. I am also thankful you should be with your uncle when in this humour: it will repay him for all his treatment of me."

"But, mamma," was her daughter's reply; "the fact is, that you have been so brilliant in your remarks of late, that in order to reply to you as you deserved, I have worn out my

intellect. I am like a ship after it has been
out in a heavy sea, in need of repairs, and
must make for port."

"Your metaphors are always so striking
and so poetical, dear Trichy," said Mrs.
Cadogan, "I fully expect that you will drop
into verse some day, like Mr. Wegg. It
would be such a satisfaction to think that
a child of mine is a poet,—one of the great
ones of the earth! Only think, Trichy, how
pleasant it would be were you to be called
'The nightingale of Sedgeborough.' Now
that is a pretty idea, is it not? Quite worthy
of your mother?"

"You Sedgeborough people are all so
clever, I am heartily tired of you!" went on
Beatrice. "If there is a thing I loathe, it is
a clever person. If I ever marry, my husband
shall be an imbecile."

"My unfortunate grandchildren, what a
fate will be theirs!"

" It shall be my prayer that they should inherit their father's mental incapacities."

" This is a second edition of ' Locksley Hall,' and you are going to Cadogan to de-claim about ' The dreary, dreary moorland, and the barren, barren shore.' "

" It is quite true, though, I think a clever person, an intellectual person, or even an intelligent person, is quite intolerable. Every-body in Sedgeborough has been put under a glass-frame, and has been forced into most unnatural growth."

" Pretty idea for a poem that. Let me see—

'A maid I was. Ah, well-a-day!
Doomed in Sedgeborough town to stay,
Where the good folks, like plants below,
Glass-frames were always forc'd to grow;
Which them so very clever made,
That I was cast into the shade.' "

" Is that impromptu, mamma? Since you can't be Mr. Wegg, you deserve to be his wife."

In point of fact it was a relief to Beatrice to go away from her mother for a little. Mrs. Cadogan was rather trying to those even who were most attached to her, and recognized her real kindness and good feeling. Beatrice found it a great exertion to talk and laugh when she felt inclined to be silent and commonplace. Now, her uncle merely expected her to be punctual for all meals, to say a few words about the weather during their progress, and look well at the · head of his table. He would only have been surprised had she been brilliant and witty, for he had never been accustomed to witty conversation, and did not understand its meaning. Had he heard anything of the kind, he would, probably, have reasoned with himself as follows:—He was never witty; he was a gentleman, therefore a gentleman was never witty. His bailiff and the attorney who managed his affairs sometimes perpetrated jokes, and Sir Peter considered this conduct savoured of audacity.

If, therefore, it was audacious and under-bred in his bailiff or attorney to indulge in wit in his presence, what would it not have been in his niece ?

And Beatrice really found it an exhilarating change when she was allowed to be commonplace, and do nothing more worthy of remark than find something new to say about the weather at all the different meals.

She had arrived at Cadogan on a Saturday, and the next morning she prepared to walk to church with her uncle at half-past ten. Sir Peter took his gold-headed stick and Beatrice a light cane, and they started ready to encounter the dangers of the way. If they were to meet any cow or dangerous animal, Beatrice feared, however, these weapons of defence would not be of much service. Hers was too light and small to do much execution, and she was convinced her uncle's sense of propriety would be outraged to such a degree at any animal daring to advance towards him—Sir Peter Cadogan, of Cadogan —that he would be deprived of all self-possession and power of action.

" What a pity it is," she thought, a little sadly, as they started on their walk this Sunday morning, "that cows are not re-specters of persons."

" Is Miss Dreadnought still unmarried ? " she inquired, as they passed a villa belonging to a Mr. Dreadnought, a man of good family, and much celebrity in many ways.

" She is not married ; and I would beg you to observe, Beatrice, that when young women forget to acknowledge the dictates of decorum, and the proper reticence which is incumbent on their position, they do remain —ahem—I would beg you to observe that such

young women, however great their charms,
do remain—ahem—longer unmarried than
would otherwise have been the case."

" You think, then, that Miss Dreadnought
might have been charming, if she had been
taught to restrain her speech and give up
hunting."

"I think it is distressing when a young
lady of Miss Dreadnought's position and
descent so forgets—ahem—those principles
and considerations—ahem—those principles
and considerations which should rule her
conduct.   It is—ahem — distressing when
she forgets what is due to herself."

" And her ancestors,—she should remember
her ancestors," laughed Beatrice.

" And her many noble relatives, who
cannot but be vexed that she should, without
the due thought and consideration which
might have been expected from her—ahem—
that she should ride to hounds—ahem —

seldom accompanied by a more respectable or trustworthy person than her father's groom."

Voices at that moment broke upon their ears, one of which was that of a female, pitched in a high and querulous key.

"Dread nought, Uncle Peter! We have spoken of the angel, and see her wings. Mr. Macdonald has been walking to church, and she, of course, quite by accident, came out as he passed their gates."

It was rather amusing, Beatrice thought, that this accident occurred so frequently, for every Sunday Miss Dreadnought chanced to start for church as Mr. Macdonald passed her gate.

"Perhaps," thought Beatrice, "she may be afraid of cows too, and may wish to have Mr. Macdonald's protection." It was really quite generous of her to make this excuse, for she knew well that Miss Dreadnought feared neither man nor beast.

As they came into the churchyard, the two parties joined company, and greetings were exchanged. To judge from Miss Dreadnought's appearance, no one could have believed what rumour said of her. It is true that she was of a large substantial person for a young lady who called herself two-and-twenty years of age, and she did not seem to lack physical power. But the expression of her face would have led a stranger to suppose that she was liable to the vapours of our grandmothers. She seemed hardly able to support the weight of her head,—which it must be admitted was by no means diminutive,—and would hang it first on one side and then on the other, in a fashion which had the merit of being striking, if not elegant.

Mr. Macdonald said once that she reminded him of a well-developed cabbage, for though her body was large, it looked slender in comparison to the size of her head.

For the rest, a good complexion, grey eyes, and nondescript hair, made her consider herself "lovely"; and this she was not ashamed to confess. She could not understand, for her part, how it was that every man did not fall in love with her. Mr. Macdonald, on the other hand, could understand it very well, though she walked to church with him every Sunday.

In fact, her carelessness as to her use or abuse of language, her hunting and shooting, seldom fascinated men, though she amused them. She herself felt at times that the life she led was hardly satisfactory, and would say occasionally that she would like to give up her hunting horses, keep a carriage, and act more in accordance with the ideas of other people. If it is a virtue to be free from pride, she was certainly virtuous in this matter. She rather liked men to call her "Jem," her real name being Jemima, and she would have talked as much and as readily to Sir Peter's coachman as to Sir Peter himself. Sir Peter spoke of her faults with severity; but had so often said that a young woman in her position should act differently, that he had convinced himself that this position was very high. It was, moreover, a point of fact, that she was well-descended, could count several titled names among those of her relations, and had occasionally visited at noble houses. Sir Peter, therefore, could not fail to be inspired with a great respect for her position, and this respect was gradually reflected on Miss Dreadnought herself. There is something very charming to an elderly widower in a young face, even though it be of the longest, which smiles on him as readily as on a younger man; for if Miss Dreadnought

walked to church with Mr. Macdonald, she
as regularly walked back from church with
Sir Peter, and talked to him in the prettiest
manner conceivable, and as though she had
been a bread-and-butter girl of seventeen,
who had never ridden to hounds in her life.

Beatrice, following her uncle and Miss
Dreadnought with Mr. Macdonald, noticed
the modulations in the tones of their voices,
as well as the pretty and youthful gestures
perpetrated by the lady, and thought to
herself that Cadogan would not long be a
second home for her to come to whenever
she was tired of her own. Miss Dreadnought
she knew would, if she ever came to be
Lady Cadogan, invite her for a stiff and
occasional visit to the hall, and would do
her the honours of her establishment with
marked condescension. But Miss Cadogan
felt it would be wormwood and gall to her
to be treated with marked condescension by

Miss Dreadnought, to whom she had con-descended in her day, as mistress of her uncle's house. Then, also, she might, in the course of nature, cease to be Miss Cadogan by courtesy, for the real Miss Cadogan might come to take her own position in society.

Beatrice was glad when, as they stopped at the villa gates, her uncle refused all invi-tations to go in; but, turning to Mr. Mac-donald, asked him to lunch at Cadogan, saying he would take him round the farm afterwards, and let him see some prize bullocks. Mr. Macdonald, who had bullocks of his own, expressed himself happy to come to lunch, and see those of Sir Peter, while Beatrice indulged in surmises as to what there was in going round a farm which should make it so essentially an employment for a Sunday afternoon. She knew that she had a pleasant sense of her own virtue, and of doing her duty as a British citizen, when she put on her thick boots, and accompanied her uncle in these walks.

Miss Cadogan was not, however, destined to have her usual quiet Sunday walk. In the first place, Mr. Macdonald talked and laughed, so that she was obliged to talk and laugh also, unmindful of her uncle's presence. In the second place, she followed her uncle into the cowhouse, and saw Mr. Macdonald feeling and pinching the beasts with the air of a connoisseur. She was seized with an eager desire to show her own familiarity with the pursuits of a country life. She was not obliged to advance far to obtain her object, which was a great encouragement to proceed, for in the stall nearest the door two calves were stabled.

She took a last glance to see the way Mr. Macdonald pinched the bullocks, and, as he looked business-like, and as though he understood all about the matter, she determined to give her calf just such another. She walked up the stall fearlessly—so fearlessly, indeed, that she chose the larger of the two on which to prove her knowledge of these affairs.

Mr. Macdonald and Sir Peter were stopped in their quiet and stately progress by the sound of distracted cries for help coming from the distance.

"Gracious Heaven!" cried the baronet, and, as on another occasion which has been recorded, he dropped his lower jaw and his delicately-poised eye-glass. He stood motionless in the centre of the way, so that Mr. Macdonald had much difficulty in passing him to hasten to Miss Cadogan's assistance. Sir Peter said again, with slow articulation,

"Gracious Heaven!"

Beatrice had pinched her calf with fingers which, though white and slender, were not devoid of strength; and the calf, excited by

R

such unusual and extraordinary treatment, turned round upon her in self-protection, and kicked and buffeted her against the wall. "Help!" cried Miss Cadogan, "help!"—and, seizing her cane, she dealt blows of no doubtful significance on the back of the unfortunate and duly-incensed animal, which was preparing itself for a more terrible onslaught, when Mr. Macdonald came to the assistance of both it and its antagonist. When extricated, Miss Cadogan announced, with solemnity, "She would never touch one of these beastly creatures as long as she lived."

"But why did you choose a calf?" cried Mr. Macdonald, no longer able to restrain his amusement.

"Do you think it would have been better had I done it to a developed calf?" she asked, with indignation. "I should have been killed outright, that is all." She had gone out into the courtyard as she said this, and had seated herself on a wheelbarrow, to gain breath and composure, when the baronet joined them.

"Beatrice," he said, with severity and dignity, "I must—ahem—must beg you to preserve—ahem—the amenities of life."

"I am sure I wish your calves would," she said, joining in Mr. Macdonald's laughter.

"You have startled and surprised me," he began again.

"But, dear me! I think I should have startled and surprised you more had I not called for help, and you had found a corpse, not yet cold, on your return. Mr. Macdonald, you are a barbarian to laugh," she continued, turning on him with warmth; "consider the possibilities of the case!"

"Suppose that we conduct—ahem—conduct Miss Cadogan to the house."

So Beatrice was conducted to the house.

"Good-bye, Mr. Macdonald," she said; "and let me inform you that the way you ridiculed my distress was shameful."

"Let me advise you, as a friend, not to pinch calves again," was his answer.

CHAPTER III.

"Man meets with man at leisure and at ease :
We to our neighbours and our equals come."

On the seventh day of Beatrice's visit to
Cadogan, there was a large dinner-party—
one of those pompous affairs at which, she
said, everybody looked like a well-regulated
machine, which consumed as much food and
uttered as many words as were expected,
and no more.

Very stately and dignified Sir Peter looked,
and very charming and self-possessed his
niece looked, as they received their guests.

Beatrice was taken in to dinner by a Lord
Alfred Darlington, who seemed infinitely to
prefer the pleasures of the table to the

pleasures of conversation. She could make
allowances for this sort of thing, as she, too,
was quite capable of enjoying the entrées,
entremets, and dry sherry provided; but
still she thought Lord Alfred carried his
attention to these things too far.

She turned, therefore, to her other neighbour, who proved to be much more amusing.
He told her, in the most pleasant and contented manner conceivable, that the country
had gone to the dogs, and that he had said
so long ago.

"We'll have a revolution," he said, smiling, as he quaffed his champagne. "When
these Republicans have sent all the trade
from the country, they'll have to rise to find
some employment." And, beaming over his
cotelettes à la soubise, he descanted on what
he should do were he in power. He would
put an end to strikes with a high hand; he
would send troops of soldiers among all mal-

contents, with orders to spare no one, young or old, woman or child.

"It does not matter, you know, if all whom you kill are to blame. Just shoot down a few, and the discontented will be frightened."

"You should become a Member of Parliament, Mr. Ditchley," said Beatrice, who had found this conversation very enlivening.

"Oh, no," he said, deprecatingly, but thinking that this was a very charming girl, who could recognize merit when she saw it. "Oh, no, I don't think of that; but if I were to go to Parliament, I should soon let people know what I thought about matters."

"I am sure your system of government would be delightful. You would put everybody out of the way who inconvenienced us or interfered with our comfort."

"I'd soon put an end to the present state

of affairs, at any rate; but as it is we shall all be murdered in our beds some of these days. I may not live to see it," he said, smiling pleasantly, "but you will, you will."

In the drawing-room, after dinner, the ladies talked in gentle, moderate tones about their children, their houses, their servants, and their neighbours, satisfied as long as they could patter out their words without long pauses, and never dreaming of saying anything new or interesting. They did not want sense, but only talk; and had any of their number attempted to give them new ideas, they would probably have considered her upsetting and troublesome.

Miss Dreadnought talked in querulous, drawling tones of camellias, cinerarias, and other greenhouse plants, of her adoration of ferns, and the beauty of the advancing spring, in a manner which would have warranted any stranger in denying the truth of the accusations against her.

Beatrice gave old Mrs. Melville a glowing description of her Sunday's adventure, who said to her, with the greatest earnestness, "My dear, you should never do things like that. It is all very well to go with your uncle to the cows, and very nice, I am sure, but you should take care of yourself. A young girl should never expose herself to any unnecessary difficulty."

Sir Peter, when he came to the drawing-room, went up to Miss Dreadnought at once, and Beatrice noticed how pleased he seemed to be with her conversation, and, listening, heard that she talked to him about a new pelargonium; so that she questioned herself as to what there could be in pelargoniums to make them a subject so eminently adapted for a young lady to descant on.

"If Mr. Macdonald were to talk to my

uncle about pelargoniums, he would be thought troublesome and foolish "; and, again, " I wonder if Major Aylmer would have liked me better had I spoken to him about the fullness, richness, and beauty of a flower of which ' dear Lady Duncar' is so fond." Then she came to the conclusion that it must be the aristocratic name, and not the pelargonium, which was so full of interest for her uncle.

Occasionally, during the course of the evening, young ladies would be induced to go to the piano and sing; but Beatrice noticed that their music was entirely mechanical. They sang of love, despair, and sorrow, with an easy, well-bred, self-satisfied grace that was very charming. She supposed, from what she knew of them, that they would have considered it quite improper to have put depth of expression into the words of a love-song. When Miss Dreadnought went to the piano, Beatrice felt some curiosity as to what she would sing, and was surprised to hear her warble forth, with a happy face,

"Tears, idle tears, I know not what ye mean;
Tears from the depth of some divine despair
Rise to the heart and gather to the eyes
On looking on the happy autumn fields,
And thinking of the days that are gone by."

As Beatrice had no desire that the county big-wigs and their ladies should consider her improper, she determined, when she was asked to go to the piano, to sing a song in which she could retain the happiness of her expression with reason.

"A very pleasant party," said Sir Peter, with self-satisfaction, when his guests had gone. "I am quite glad, my dear, to have been enabled to show you a little—ahem—a little good society. Whenever you come here, I shall make an effort—ahem—for your advantage, to see some of my friends, as on this occasion. Very superior man, Lord Alfred Darlington!"

"He eat as though he had not seen food for a week, and is very silent," said Beatrice.

"Perhaps he may be silent with you, my dear, since—ahem—you are not—ahem—so conversant with the topics of society as— ahem—ahem—the lady who sits at the head of my table usually is—Miss Dreadnought."

"Does she usually sit at the head of your table?" asked Beatrice, raising her eyebrows.

"If you would kindly allow me to proceed"—

"Well, uncle, what of Miss Dreadnought?"

"Miss Dreadnought, who is accustomed— ahem—to move in the best circles, informs me that—ahem—Lord Alfred Darlington is an exceedingly superior young man."

"But there are many kinds of superiority. There is a superiority of mind or of morals, a superiority of rank and position, and a

superiority of appetite; to which latter Lord
Alfred has, no doubt, many claims."

"Beatrice," said her uncle, in tones of grave
reproof, "I am distressed to be compelled
by duty—ahem—by duty, to inform you that
you have—ahem—shown a carelessness in
your actions and words during the last few
days of which—ahem—I cannot approve."

Beatrice laughed a little, for the only way
she had ever displeased her uncle before was
by her misfortune and adventure on the
Sunday previous.

On going to her room, she found lying on
the table a letter from her mother, which had
come by the evening's post. It ran as
follows:—

"Dear Trichy,—You must come home to-
morrow; you are engaged to dine at the
Aylmers', at seven o'clock. I was at the
Murrays' last night, and met Miss Evans for
the first time. They say that she is clever,

and I suppose that talent must therefore consist in a short memory, as the only remarkable thing I could discover about her was that she had forgotten the body of her gown. She coughed once during dinner, and I took the opportunity to offer her a lace shawl of my own. This she declined, under the impression that she was warmly clothed. What a revelation it must have been when she looked in her glass on her return home! Young Mr. Willoughby was seated beside me, and I do not know what horrified him most, my charity or her forgetfulness! It is quiet true that Florence Aylmer has the Stuart mania.

" Your affectionate parent,

" S. Cadogan.

" Thursday, Sedgeborough."

Beatrice was much surprised by the contents of this letter. She knew her mother was perfectly serious, and that, whatever her own inclinations might be, she must return home. But what could her mother's motive be?

Beatrice puzzled long over this question, and could not find any answer to it. "What waste of money," she thought, "to let me come here for only a week. And shall I ever come back again under the same pleasant circumstances? I should have liked to have stayed on, and had a little fight with Miss Dreadnought. It would have been so exhilarating; and, besides, I believe I should have been the victor. Possession is nine-tenths of the law; and I, having possession of my uncle, would not let him escape from me easily."

It was not, however, for her own sake merely that she regretted the fascination which she saw Miss Dreadnought was beginning to exercise over Sir Peter. Beatrice was sincerely attached to her uncle, notwithstanding his pompous manners and words,

and did not believe that a marriage with
Miss Dreadnought would be conducive to
his happiness. As Lady Cadogan, she believed that Miss Dreadnought would drop all
the artificial appearance of innocence, and
all those pretty ways which she put on now
to charm the old man; that she would in
many ways wound his self-love and the
sense of propriety which was to him the
dearest thing on earth. She would have
power over him, and would use it, not to
contribute to his happiness, but to that of
herself and her own friends. Sir Peter
would see this, and at the same time would
not have strength enough of character and
resolution to put an end to it, and exert his
own authority.

CHAPTER IV.

"Her fair form may stand and shine,
   Make bright our days, and light our dreams;
Turning to scorn, with lips divine,
   The falsehood of extremes."—TENNYSON.

   "Aug' mein aug' was sinkst du nieder?
   Goldne Träume, kommt ihr wieder?
   Weg du Traum! so gold du bist
   Hier auch Lieb' und Leben ist."—GÖTHE.

   "Der edle Mensch
   Sey hülfreich und gut!
   Unermüdet schaff' er
   Das Nützliche, Rechte."—GÖTHE.

FLORENCE AYLMER had known that the day-dream of her life was over when she and Ernest had separated after their return from visiting Mrs. Blake.

But hers was not a nature in which love took the form of passion, which, when it is disappointed, throws a veil of darkness over the world. She did not beat out her sorrow in despair, or storm Heaven with her cries. She went about as usual, satisfied Miss Frost with her studies, her mother and sisters by her interest in other matters. If her courage gave way, it was only for the space of a moment, when she would bow her head with a bitter cry, or her eyes would fill unaccountably with tears when she had seemed to be engrossed in some employment.

This sorrow could never have taken a positive form had it not been for the letter which Ernest had written, and in which he had told her that he loved her, in express terms; for there is a certain pride and restraint natural to women which forbid them to admit their love, even to themselves, until they have been told that they are loved.

It was well for Florence that she soon

found relief in work, and that of a kind, moreover, which she knew would have been acceptable to Ernest.

Anne Stuart had frequently offered to take her about with her, so that she might see the kind of employment she had; and Florence now asked her to do this. But it needed very short experience to prove to her that she could neither teach at a Sunday-school nor preach at mother's meetings. She could not attend sewing societies for home or foreign missions, during which the ladies assembled entertained each other by religious gossip, which appeared to her even in worse taste than the gossip which they would have characterized as worldy. She then remembered Miss Mabberely, a friend of her mother's, who, being of independent means and advanced years, devoted her life to work among the poor of Sedgeborough, and had once said to the Aylmers, " If any of you

get tired of enjoying yourselves, you can
come to me." She had taken a room in one
of the poorest parts of the town, and here
she kept a school for children who would
otherwise have been allowed to grow up on
the streets as best they might. Miss Mabberely was gifted with a decided and ener-
getic character; so that, though the number
of her scholars was fluctuating, she held her
school, on the whole, well together. She
had hitherto had no assistance in these under-
takings, as most of the ladies of Sedgeborough seemed to agree with Mrs. Cadogan,
who had said, frankly, "I believe in the
Articles of my Church, which plainly condemn all works of supererogation, as proceeding from the Evil One." And those few who
did desire to be useful in their day preferred to put themselves under the direction
of the clergy.

"They need the presence of black coats to

encourage them, poor things," Miss Mabberely said; "and it is just as well they
should be conscious of their weakness, and
go where they may be of some service. In
some land, you know, the worms would
destroy the crops if it were not for the crows.
I don't like crows myself, but no doubt they
are frequently useful. We all have our fail-
ings, and Heaven forbid I should ridicule
those of my sisters!"

Florence and Lizzie had often gone to this
school of Miss Mabberely's, and had been
pleased and amused by what they had seen;
and so, in her present difficulty, Florence
determined to apply to Miss Mabberely, aware
that her mother would approve of any work
done in connexion with her.

Miss Mabberely was glad to accept Florence's
offer of help, for she had often found the
numbers of her pupils made it impossible to
preserve even an appearance of order; and,

besides this, she felt that to have sympathy
in her work would be an encouragement to
herself.

"You must not expect to find it a pleasant or enlivening occupation," she said to
Florence. "You will have many head-
aches and disappointments, and will find
the children dirty, disobedient, and unruly.
You must expect that no sooner have you
fixed your affections on one child, and got
it to learn something, than an evil impulse
will seize it, and make it stay away until it
has forgotten everything. Or it may be
that it will take measles; after which it will
be useless to attempt to teach it at all. I
have found there is nothing like an attack
of measles for depriving children of the small
amount of brains given them by Nature. If
you can make up your mind to these sort of
occurrences, I shall be most happy to have
you."

Florence smiled, as she replied the idea did not seem very encouraging, but that she could make up her mind to it; so that it was arranged that Florence should spend three hours of every morning with her.

It was to this that Mrs. Cadogan referred, in her letter to Beatrice, when she said that Florence was touched by the Stuart mania. She did not at all approve of the affair, and she told Mrs. Aylmer so plainly; but then, when was Mrs. Cadogan not plain in her speech?

"I can understand it when there is a clergyman in the case; but when there is nothing of the kind, it appears to me most unhealthy. It is one of the signs of the times. Why cannot a young lady be contented to stay in her father's house; and if she must have work, why should she not make his shirts and sew on his buttons?" she asked.

"Mrs. Cadogan, did you ever make a shirt for your father?" inquired Mr. Aylmer.

"No; but had I been able to stay in his house, I should not have wished for any work, as I should have been satisfied to spend my days, as a young lady ought, in talking, walking, reading, and playing a little music. You see I had to be a governess, and had therefore to read a good deal and play a great deal."

"Florence's occupation is very innocent," went on Mr. Aylmer; "and not in the least one which will make her strong-minded, in the bad sense of the word. Lois and Miss Frost walk with her to Miss Mabberely's school every morning, and Miss Mabberely walks back with her to the gardens, through which she comes herself, and so reaches home without having been in the streets alone, which, I am aware, is considered a shocking impropriety."

Mrs. Sidmouth also expressed disapproval of Florence's conduct in this matter. " A young girl should have plenty of employment in her father's house and in her own occupations, without running about the world in search of work," she said, and shook her head with grave solemnity.

" But, Mrs. Sidmouth," replied Florence, to whom these remarks had been personally addressed, " I do not fly about the world in search of work. I inquired, and found that there was work ready at hand, and in doing it I surely am not to blame. It is not pleasant, I admit, but I hope it soon may become so."

" My dear, do you not remember what Pascal said—so very truly—that many, many of the evils of life are created ' by a man's being unable to sit still in his own room.' "

" Yes, I do remember, and think he is right in this as far as it goes. I should be much to blame were I to create work, or blindly attempt that for which I have not sufficient knowledge. No one can deprecate more than I the philanthropy which makes men, as soon as they see an evil, rush to the effect its cure, without seeing clearly also the way to do so. I do not think I can be accused of this, for I certainly know my A B C, and have to teach very little more than this."

"Ah! Philanthropy, like Hester's—I know," and Mrs. Sidmouth nodded and looked very meaning. "She rushes at a man, takes him by the throat, and declares he shall become a good citizen and Christian, whether he will or not." Mrs. Sidmouth, in saying this, acted the part she supposed her niece to play with great force and energy. She stretched out her hand, seized her imaginary man, and shook him with great heartiness and goodwill.

Her daughter Charlotte, who had been present during this discussion, here closed her book, gave utterance to a melancholy groan, and, paying no heed to her mother's theatrical start and exclamation, said, " If I were only rich, Florence, I should pay for the education of these unfortunate pupils of yours by some good and orthodox Christian. It is sad to think how their infant minds will be perverted."

Florence answered, " I am sure Miss Mabberely would be delighted if you did."

Lizzie once or twice went with her sister, and Miss Mabberely, on these occasions, insisted on giving her work also among the children. " They are so dirty," objected Lizzie.

" You can get soap and water, I suppose, when you go home," said Miss Mabberely; adding, " you are much more suited for this kind of thing than Florence. Her intellect

is of too abstracted and refined a nature ever
to understand the tricks and fashions of
children. Nor can she impress her ideas on
them with such force as we can. If we had
only a number of men and women here, she
would give them a first-rate lecture on
science or ethics."

In point of fact, it was very hard and
unsatisfactory work for Florence. She found
the greatest difficulty in making the children
understand her or in gaining any influence
over their minds. It is to her credit, however, that she determined to persevere.

I suppose it must have been, unconsciously,
some encouragement to her to know that
Ernest Stuart would probably hear what she
was doing, and might either be led to judge
less severely or to question the justice of his
judgments. She had never heard his name
mentioned by his sisters since his departure,
for they never supposed that she could be

in the least interested to hear of him, and she could not trust herself to ask any question, however unimportant. She would not have heard much, even had she asked, for Ernest had never been a good correspondent; and now the short letter that they had received, had merely announced his arrival in London, and gave none of those seemingly unimportant details in which women take so great a delight.

END OF VOL I.

PRINTED BY E. J. FRANCIS, TOOK's COURT, CHANCERY LANE, E.C.

PUTTYPUT'S PROTÉGÉE;

Or, ROAD, RAIL, AND RIVER.

A Humorous Story, in Three Books.

By HENRY GEORGE CHURCHILL.

Read about Lord Maresfield, the Philanthropist.
Read about Lady Maresfield, the Peerless Peeress.
Read about Obadiah Puttyput, the Good-hearted Quaker.
Read about Bob Bembrow's Laughable Adventures.
Read about Lucy Pottley, the " P.D."
Read about Mabel Waldegrave, Mr. Puttyput's Protégée.
Read about Peter Pallwole, the Portmanteauist.
Read about Sir George Talbot, the Returned Convict.
Read about Slitherem Slaberdash, the ex-Tallow-Chandler.
Read about Louey Melville, his Wonderful Legacy.
Read about Theophilus Cutshort's Fatherly Actions.
Read about Coney, the Comical Bird-catcher.
Read about Dollops's Mysterious Fourpence.
Read about George Waldegrave's Trip to India.
Read about Polly Scollop, from Miss Techum's.
Read about Mrs. Botherem, the Pattern Housekeeper.
Read about Jane, Tom, Bob, Sam, Bill, Jo, and Jehoshaphat,
    the Happy Family.
Read about Maria Pallwole, the Suffering Mother.
Read about the Twin Idiots, Her Offspring.
Read about Mr. Duse, of Stale Wharf.
Read about Dawley and Foster, the Gentlemanly Villains.
Read about Lord Upperten, the Traveller.
Read about Blanche Duprez, the Governess.
Read about Blue Peter, the ex-Pugilist.
Read about the Devonsherry Brothers' Rope Trick.
Read about Farmer Bleak and his Three Daughters.
Read

PUTTYPUT'S PROTÉGÉE;

Or, Road, Rail, and River.

SAMUEL TINSLEY, 34, Southampton Street, Strand.